THE GHOST OF DROWNED MEADOW

KELLEY SKOVRON

THE GHOST OF DROWNED MEADOW

Scholastic Inc.

Copyright © 2022 by Kelley Skovron

All rights reserved. Published by Scholastic Inc., *Publishers since 1920.* SCHOLASTIC and associated logos are trademarks and/or registered trademarks of Scholastic Inc.

The publisher does not have any control over and does not assume any responsibility for author or third-party websites or their content.

No part of this publication may be reproduced, stored in a retrieval system, or transmitted in any form or by any means, electronic, mechanical, photocopying, recording, or otherwise, without written permission of the publisher. For information regarding permission, write to Scholastic Inc., Attention: Permissions Department, 557 Broadway, New York, NY 10012.

This book is a work of fiction. Names, characters, places, and incidents are either the product of the author's imagination or are used fictitiously, and any resemblance to actual persons, living or dead, business establishments, events, or locales is entirely coincidental.

ISBN 978-1-338-75432-2

10 9 8 7 6 5 4 3 2 1   22 23 24 25 26

First edition, September 2022

Printed in the U.S.A. 40

Book design by
Christopher Stengel

In loving memory of my father, Richard C. Skovron.

CHAPTER

ONE

The first time it happened, Morgan Calvino was rereading one of her favorite Japanese light novels, *My Secret Dream of a Boring Life, Volume 1.* She was stretched out on her bed, a half-full can of coconut seltzer on the small table beside her. A cool evening breeze drifted in through the open window, tickling her bare shins and feet.

This was probably the seventh or eighth time that Morgan had read the first volume of *My Secret Dream of a Boring Life* by Sensō Tori. She'd begun just after dinner, and was already at chapter four, where the protagonist, Zophia Zye the Night Queen, magically disguises herself as a human so that she can travel among them without frightening anyone. Naturally she brings along her loyal frost spirit, Zsa Zsa, who is now disguised as an adorable white kitten.

This chapter was one of Morgan's favorites in the whole series. Zophia and Zsa Zsa are walking through the forest, still adjusting to their new human and cat forms, when they are set upon by a pack of wolflings. Of course, such pitiful monsters are nothing compared to the power of the Night Queen, but the human adventurer Kosuke and his friends happen along and mistakenly think she needs their help.

He was slim, with shaggy black hair, refined features, and an earnest expression.

"Hey, miss! Can you use a sword?"

I wasn't sure what he was getting at.

"Yes, I have had some instruction in swordsmanship . . ."

"Great! Feel free to help out!"

Then he tossed a small sword at my feet.

TAP

I looked down at the blade. It was easily the most pathetic weapon I'd ever seen. The well maintained. The binding was frayed, and the flimsy steel was edged with rust.

Then I looked back at the human, who was smiling innocently at me.

"He's serious," I muttered to Zsa Zsa. "He actually thinks he's helping me."

"So it would seem, my queen."

TAP

"And now he's waiting for . . . gratitude?"

"That would be traditional under the circumstances as he understands them, Your Majesty."

"We shall see how well this human understands the circumstances once I turn this entire meadow to ash!"

TAP

Morgan closed her book. What *was* that tapping sound? It was like the steady annoying drip from a faucet, except coming from outside her window.

She leaned across her bed and looked out into the darkness. It wasn't raining. In fact, the purple night sky was completely clear. So where was the sound coming from?

Then she realized that the tapping had stopped.

She peered across the street to the moonlit harbor. She could just make out yachts dotting the black, rippling water. She could hear the faint *ting* of the rope lines that knocked against their aluminum masts as the boats swayed in the wind. She could hear the distant bark of a dog. But she no longer heard the dripping sound.

"Weird . . ."

She leaned back into her bed, fluffed her pillow, then opened the book to where she'd left off. It was the first meeting between Zophia Zye the Night Queen and Kosuke the human. Since Morgan knew how close the two characters would become in later volumes, she really enjoyed going back and laughing at how awkward they were together at first.

The thing was, Kosuke didn't realize that Zophia was the Night Queen in disguise, so he was just treating her like she was a regular human girl. And even though Zophia was trying to *act* like a regular human girl, she didn't really know how to do that yet, so she kept getting offended that she wasn't being given the proper respect:

I decided I would show this foolish human just how much of an insult his pathetic sword was. I began to cast the tenth-tier spell Incandescent Blaze of Lava's Birth. My hands rose to form the intricate movements, and my mouth opened to speak the prayer of Kagutsuchi the fire god.

TAP

"I hate to interrupt when you are in such a beautifully righteous rage, my queen," Zsa

Zsa said mildly. "But I suspect that once you cast a spell in the lost language of the gods, this human and his companions will no longer believe you to be one of them, and everything we have done to get to this point will have been for naught."

TAP

"But I can't just let him think he's saving me," I protested. "As though I'm some helpless—"

TAP

"Okay, *seriously . . .*" Morgan groaned as she once more closed her book and looked out the window. The sky remained clear.

The sound was incredibly annoying. But where was it coming from? A dripping air-conditioning unit, maybe? But it wasn't hot enough for that anymore. And now that she thought about it, this house had central heating and air, so window AC units weren't even a thing around here.

Maybe she was just hearing things. After all, she still hadn't gotten used to how quiet it was out on Long Island. In Brooklyn there had always been background noise. Cars, buses, trains, horns honking, people shouting, alarms going off. It had all mixed together into a steady drone that she could wrap around herself like a cozy blanket. She hadn't realized how comforting it had been until she lost it. Now it was one of the many things she missed since moving out of the city.

Not that Port Jefferson wasn't nice. The harbor was pretty, with all its fancy sailboats bobbing around. The nearby downtown was cute, with little shops and restaurants. She also liked having a house instead of a tiny apartment. And she had to admit that in general, things smelled a whole lot better. But she even missed some of those Brooklyn smells, like the food from old Mr. Zhao's restaurant on the corner.

Morgan sighed and turned back to her book. At least she still had the Night Queen. She gazed down at the manga-style illustration on the cover, which showed Zophia Zye in her true oni form: tall, regal, with blue skin and long, white, jagged hair. She wore an elegant black gown and a cape with a high collar. Morgan didn't think it was possible for someone to be cooler or more beautiful in this world or any other than the Night Queen.

Of course, Morgan had already read all ten books in the *My Secret Dream of a Boring Life* series, and the manga adaptation as well. But since the move to Long Island, she'd found that rereading those books, especially the first few volumes, made her feel a little less lonely.

She was just getting ready to dive back into the world of the Night Queen when she heard her mother's voice from the doorway.

"Don't forget it's a school night."

Marissa Zeggini was medium height, with dark wavy hair like Morgan's and the piercing gaze of a trial lawyer. She'd changed out of her suit after dinner and now wore a comfy set of yellow pajamas. Her arms were folded across her chest and one eyebrow was raised. What she was really saying was, *Don't you think it's time to go to bed?*

Morgan sighed. "I know, I know."

She closed the window, put her book on the bedside table, and slid under her covers.

Her mother came in and gave her a kiss on the forehead. "Good night, sweetie."

"Did you hear a loud dripping sound?" Morgan asked.

Her mother frowned. "When?"

"Just now."

Her mom tucked her in, even though she didn't need it. "Sometimes when you feel lonely, your mind plays tricks on you."

"I'm not lonely," Morgan protested, even though she definitely was.

Her mother smiled gently and smoothed Morgan's hair back from her forehead. "Morgan, sweetie, maybe if you tried a little harder to make friends at school, you'd feel better."

"I *do* try. It's just that nobody's into the same stuff that I'm into. All they ever talk about is clothes and boys and wakeboarding. I don't even know what wakeboarding *is*."

"It's like waterskiing, but with a board instead of skis," her mom said. "It's actually a lot of fun."

"Well, I've never done it, and they all have."

"I'm sure you'll find things you have in common with them if you give them a chance. Maybe some of them even like that Night Queen series you love so much."

Morgan gave her mother a long, slow eye roll to show just how unlikely that was.

Her mother shrugged. "Hey, you never know. They might just not obsess over it all the time like you and Madison."

"I guess . . ."

Morgan didn't want to talk about Madison. She didn't want to *think* about that traitor. Madison said they'd always be best friends no matter what, but she hadn't responded to Morgan's texts in *weeks*. Morgan's mom said she might just be busy with the beginning of school, but Morgan knew better. If Madison had time to post memes on the Night Queen chat server, she had time to talk to her "best friend." But since Morgan didn't live in Brooklyn anymore, maybe she wasn't worth the effort now.

"Morgan, I know this move hasn't been easy for you," her mom said. "But that's all the more reason to try your hardest. I promise, once you have some friends, you'll love this place. You just need to make the effort."

It was true that Morgan hadn't tried all that hard to fit in with the girls at her new school, mostly because they seemed dumb and boring. But maybe her mom was right. Maybe she wasn't giving them a chance.

"Okay, fine. Tomorrow, I'll try for real."

If nothing else, maybe she'd stop hearing things.

TWO

Zophia Zye the Night Queen and her faithful servant Zsa Zsa knew almost nothing about humans when they first visited the human realm. But because they met Kosuke so early in their adventures, it wasn't a huge problem. He was always there to help them learn how to fit in.

Sadly Morgan hadn't met anyone as nice as Kosuke on her first day, so adapting to the culture of Port Jefferson Middle School had proved to be difficult. Part of the problem, she knew, was that she was a little awkward. She didn't know what to say a lot of the time.

The first few days she didn't really talk to anyone, and every day after it felt a little more daunting to break that ice. Before classes began, she sat at her desk in homeroom and read her book. At lunch, she ate her sandwich alone and read her book. Maybe it was silly, but she'd had this fantasy that someone would see her reading, and that's all it would take: *You're a Night Queen fan? Cool, me too!*

But nope. Nobody talked about it, or even seemed to know what it was.

The other problem was that Port Jeff Middle was a lot smaller than her school in Brooklyn, and as far as she could tell, the other kids had all grown up together. Her classmates had known one another since forever, and probably so had their parents and grandparents too. Nobody was looking to make a new friend because nobody needed one. There weren't even any cool loner types like she'd seen in books and shows.

Why was real life always so disappointing?

When she walked into the lunchroom that day, she felt a strong desire to claim her usual table in the corner and plunge back into the Night Queen's far less disappointing world. But she had resolved to try harder to make friends. So she forced herself to sit at the same table as some of the girls from her class.

Of course they were talking about wakeboarding.

"This might be the last good weekend for it," Hannah was saying.

Hannah Meyer seemed to be the leader of this little group. She had suntanned skin and brown hair with lighter streaks that seemed so natural they came either from the sun or a really fancy hair salon. She had an athletic build and the confidence to go with it.

"Can your dad take us out, Hannah?" asked Piper.

Piper Morrison had long, straight blond hair and was really pretty. She probably could have been a model, except she was always hunched over and nervous, which kind of ruined it.

Hannah shook her head. "I already asked my dad. He said he has to go into the city tomorrow."

"I'll ask my mom," said Tressa. "I bet she'd take us out."

Tressa Witherspoon was one of the few Black kids in their class. She had short kinky hair that fanned out in a cool way, and one time Morgan had seen her doodling anime characters in a notebook, so she thought there might be friendship potential. But as far as she could tell, Tressa hadn't even noticed Morgan's existence.

So Morgan was genuinely surprised when Tressa suddenly turned to her.

"Hey, new girl. You're from Brooklyn, right? Do they have wakeboarding in Brooklyn?"

My name is Morgan Calvino, which you should know, considering we've been in every class together for weeks now, she thought. But tempting as that was to say, this was her chance to get into the conversation, and a snotty reply would not help.

"Uh, no, I've never been wakeboarding," she said instead. "But I hear it's fun."

"Wait." Piper looked stunned. "Like, never-never?"

"Yeah . . ."

Morgan was hoping this might prompt them to invite her along. But no.

"Anyway," said Hannah. "Tress, ask your mom after school and text us."

"Yup," said Tressa. "Should I invite Jake and them?"

"But the boys always clown around," protested Piper.

Tressa grinned at her. "They're just trying to impress you."

Piper only nervously rubbed her arms and frowned down at her veggie wrap.

"It might be the last weekend," said Hannah. "You should invite them."

There was a pause in the conversation that would have been the perfect moment to invite Morgan as well. But instead they started talking about what they would wear, since the boys were coming. Morgan tried to pay attention, but some of the boys weren't in their class so she was only sort of able to follow it.

Then Hannah said, "Oh, you know who I saw last night at the yacht club? Joel Applebaum."

"No way," said Tressa. "Is he still a creepy weirdo?"

"He's homeschooled now, so what do you think?" Hannah turned to Morgan. "Hey, new girl, don't you live near him?"

"Who?"

Piper gave Morgan a sympathetic look. "Oh, that sucks."

"*What* sucks?" Morgan asked, starting to get worried.

"Don't freak the girl out," Tressa told them. Then she turned back to Morgan. "He's harmless. If he ever tries to talk to you, just ignore him and he'll go away."

"Is there . . . something wrong with him?"

"Other than being a creepy weirdo?" asked Hannah. "No, I guess not. Have fun hanging out with him."

"Uh . . ." Morgan didn't even know how to respond to that.

"If you meet him, you'll understand," said Piper.

The conversation moved on to other things, but Morgan was still stuck on Joel Applebaum. What did "creepy weirdo" even mean? Tressa said he was harmless, so at least there was that. But whatever was wrong with him, clearly she would have to avoid him if she wanted to be friends with these girls.

CHAPTER

THREE

Volume two of My Secret Dream of a Boring Life was a lot of fun. Zophia Zye and Zsa Zsa, still in disguise as human and kitten, had joined Kosuke's adventuring party, although they had to make sure they didn't give themselves away. Sometimes they would get confused about human behavior, but Zophia could usually pass that off as being a foreigner who didn't know local customs. Other times, they would all be on a quest together, and Zophia would accidentally display too much of her incredible power, and it was funny to watch her try to cover her mistakes.

But in the end, it was actually Zsa Zsa who unintentionally outed them. There was a sweet, redheaded ranger girl in their party named Akari who was obsessed with kitten Zsa Zsa. Toward the end of the book, there was a scene where it appeared as though Zsa Zsa was in danger, and Akari completely freaked out because she still thought he was a helpless kitten:

> We hadn't counted on the harpies outflanking us. One snuck in behind, grabbed Zsa Zsa by his fluffy white scruff with her talons, then swooped into the air.
>
> "Zsa Zsa!" Akari screamed in panic.
>
> Whether Zsa Zsa was willing to admit it or not, I was certain that he had grown fond of the red-haired human. A mere harpy posed little threat to an elder frost spirit, even in kitten form. So it was probably the frightened tone in Akari's voice as she shouted his name that caused him to overreact.

TAP

His kitten shape transformed in an instant, and the now-terrified harpy found herself clutching a sinuous and jagged elder frost spirit.

He bared his icy teeth at the beast in a ferocious smile, then cleanly sliced her in half with a flick of his tail.

It had been so long since I'd seen my beloved Zsa Zsa in his true form that I couldn't help relishing in his majesty. He was like a miniature version of a great dragon of old. Once riled, it always took some time for him to regain calm, and it had been so long since he'd allowed himself to let loose. So he now whipped through the air, carving a gory swath through the flock of harpies. Blood and feathers rained down on us. All I could do was laugh in delight.

TAP

Once the harpies were no more, he settled grace-
fully on my shoulder.

"Well done, Zsa Zsa," I told him.

"Thank you, Your Majesty," he murmured.
"But I fear I may have made some trouble for
us."

"Oh?" I turned to the other members of our
party. They were all staring at us in astonish-
ment. "Ah yes . . . I suppose it's time for us to
finally come clean, Zsa Zsa."

I looked down at my soft human skin. Oddly,
I thought I might miss it. Just a little.

TAP

"Oh, come on!" burst out Morgan as she slapped her book down and glared at the open window, which once again showed a clear, purple night sky.

This was the big moment when Zophia finally reveals her true form to her friends, even though she was secretly worried that they would reject her when they learned that she wasn't human. Morgan should be relishing one of the most emotional moments of the entire series, but that stupid dripping sound kept distracting her.

Morgan reached up to pull the window shut, but paused when she realized the dripping had stopped.

That was fine. That's what she wanted.

Except then Morgan heard the crying.

Quiet, heartbreaking whimpers.

Right outside her window.

There was something about the keening voice that made the fine hairs on the back of her neck stand up. It wasn't loud or forceful, but it sounded broken. Like someone who had lost *everything*.

The bedroom felt cold now. Far too cold for an early September evening. She shivered as she leaned back into her bed. She held the book tight against her chest and waited for the muted sobs to stop.

But they didn't.

"H-Hello?" she called.

Then the crying paused. But the silence didn't make her feel better. It was like she could tell the person was still out there. Waiting . . .

What if someone was hurt? And right now they were out on the grass suffering? Why was she being such a scaredy-cat when someone might really need help?

That gave her the resolve to look out the window.

But there was no one there. And her room didn't feel cold anymore either.

First that dripping, now this crying? She knew she had an active imagination, but surely not even she could be imagining things *that* much.

Yet what else could it be?

She slowly closed the window, as though afraid of drawing attention to it. Now she wouldn't hear any dripping or crying, and she could finally bury herself for the rest of the evening in a world that was far better than her own.

FOUR

Morgan didn't sleep well that night. She kept having a camping nightmare, which was strange because she'd never been camping. She didn't remember much about it, except hiking forever through brush that scratched her skin and pulled at her hair. And for some reason she was carrying a ridiculously heavy backpack. Even worse, it was one of those awful nightmares that woke her up, then started again when she fell back asleep.

The next morning she awoke tired and irritable.

"Geez," her dad said when she trudged into the

kitchen. Gabe Calvino was on the short side, bald on top, with big bushy eyebrows. "Who let in the thunderclouds?"

"Blegh." She pulled the box of cereal out of the pantry and poured it into a bowl.

He grinned. "It must be difficult having an award-winning humorist for a father."

"It is a daily trial," she agreed.

Her father drew comics, but not famous ones like Superman or Spider-Man. Instead he drew an "indie" comic in which no one had powers and everyone was unhappy all the time. Yet despite all that, it was supposedly funny enough to win an Eisner Award. Her father had assured her that she'd find it funny once she was an adult. Morgan really hoped that wasn't true because she did not want to grow up to be someone who found unhappiness funny.

"Your mom had to go in to work today," her father said as he stirred sugar into his coffee. "And I've got that deadline coming up."

"So basically I'm on my own today." She slowly poured milk over her cereal.

"Well, one of the reasons we moved out here was so that you could have more autonomy. You know, go off and do stuff with your friends or whatever."

"Friends?" She grabbed a spoon and began to eat at the counter. "Ohhhh, *now* I see why people think you're so funny."

He gave her the Serious Dad look, forehead furrowed and eyes squinted with concern. "I know it's been difficult adjusting to Long Island. Your mother and I want you to know how much we appreciate everything you're doing to try to fit in."

"*Trying* is right," she said. "Trying and failing."

"You'll get there," he assured her.

"I just don't know what to *do*."

"Well, what were you planning to do today?"

She shrugged. "Read, I guess."

"Instead of staying cooped up in the house, why don't you pack a cooler with some snacks and that horrible coconut seltzer you love, and take your book down to the dock?"

"How am I going to make friends that way?" she asked.

"No idea," he said. "But it's more likely than if you stay in the house. And at least you'll be enjoying the amazing fact that we literally live across the street from the ocean now."

"Technically it's Long Island Sound," she said. "Not the ocean."

"Well, yes . . ."

"And actually not even the sound. Just a harbor that feeds into the sound."

He smiled beatifically at her. "You are a horrible child, did you know that?"

"I'm just a victim of bad parenting," she replied.

"I'm only a bad parent because your grandmother was even worse."

"I'm going to tell her you said that."

"Please don't." His smile dropped away. "Seriously, please don't."

She pretended to think about it. "*Maybe* I could forget you said it, *if* you draw me a sketch of Zophia and Zsa Zsa."

His eyebrow rose. "Another one? Seriously, how many do you need?"

"As many as I can get."

"Well, it'll have to wait until after I hit this deadline."

"Fine, but then you better put Kosuke in there too."

"You're worse than my editor," he said, then headed back to his studio.

Morgan couldn't really think of anything better to do, so she decided to take her father's advice and pack a cooler. She was nearly finished with *My Secret Dream of a Boring Life, Volume Two*, so she brought that, and volume three as well, just in case.

There was a stretch of bright green grass directly across the street from her house. The beach on the other side of the lawn was mostly rocks, broken seashells, and the occasional dead sea animal, so she couldn't just throw down a blanket and sit by the water. Instead there was a narrow pier that stretched over the water for about thirty feet to a small floating dock.

There were a few dinghies flipped upside down on the dock. Otherwise it was empty. It wasn't large enough for everyone who lived in the neighborhood to just keep their boats at the dock all the time. Instead people kept their boats on nearby moorings and rowed their dinghies back and forth. At least, that's what her father said people did. Her parents didn't have a boat, so she'd never done any of it herself. In fact, she'd never even been on a boat, unless she counted the Staten Island Ferry.

She sat down at the end of the dock with her feet dangling over the side and took out a can of coconut seltzer—which was delicious, no matter what her father said. There weren't many boats tied to their moorings right now. It was a bright sunny day, so a lot of people were probably out on the sound, fishing or wakeboarding or whatever boat people did.

Morgan wondered if Tressa and the others would go past her dock on their way out to the sound. Maybe they'd see her and invite her along. That was a thing that could happen, right? She had no idea. And she wasn't wearing a swimsuit, so she wouldn't be able to wakeboard. Should she go in and change, in case they did stop by? But what if they passed while she was inside and she completely missed them? No, better to stay here and if they invited her, she would go and just cheer them on. It wasn't like she felt a mighty need to wakeboard. She just wanted some friends.

She could picture it pretty easily. Cruising out of the harbor with the three girls, the sparkling water all around them. Hannah the jock would probably be really good. Morgan couldn't quite picture timid Piper doing surf-skiing or whatever it was. Was Tressa good? Probably, if her parents had their own boat. Maybe she could teach Morgan how to do it. By the next summer, she'd go out with them all the time, wakeboarding and whatever else these Long Island girls did. Then she supposed she would *be* a Long Island girl . . .

"Night Queen fan, huh?"

Morgan squinted up at the boy who now stood beside her. He was a lot paler than most of the Long Island kids she'd seen around, and he had shaggy black hair that curled up a little at the ends. He was wearing a T-shirt with characters from a popular anime called *Infamous Motley.*

Aha, thought Morgan. *My people.*

"Are *you* a Night Queen fan?" she asked.

"Of course," he said, like it was a ridiculous question.

He nodded down at the book in her hands. "But I haven't read the original light novels, just the mangas. Are they any different?"

"Not really," she said. "I just like them better because they get inside Zophia's head more."

"They're finally making an anime," the boy said.

"Yeah. I hope they don't mess it up too badly."

"Well, it's being produced by the same studio that did *Carrion Flowers*, and that show was amazing."

"Your parents let you watch that?"

Carrion Flowers was rated M for mature. Morgan wasn't allowed to watch those kinds of shows yet, even if they were animated. And if she was being honest with herself, she worried it was too scary anyway.

"I guess my parents don't really pay much attention to ratings stuff," the boy mused, as though he'd never thought about it either way. "But it really is an amazing story. Would your parents let you read the manga at least?"

"I'm not sure . . ." She wondered if reading the manga would be less scary. People on the Night Queen chat server *did* talk about how great it was . . .

"Well, I have all the mangas if you ever want to borrow them sometime," said the boy.

"Really?"

"Sure. I mean, we're basically neighbors." He pointed to a house a few doors down. "I'm Joel. I live right over there."

Joel.

As in Joel "creepy weirdo" Applebaum.

Suddenly Morgan hoped Tressa and the others *didn't* go past the dock. What if they saw Morgan talking to Joel? What if they thought she was *hanging out* with him? What if one of them took a picture and posted it somewhere? *New girl with bff homeschooled creepy weirdo #blessed*

That would be the end of Morgan's social life at Port Jeff Middle.

"Uh, I better get going." She hurriedly packed up her cooler.

"Oh, okay . . ." said Joel.

Morgan felt a pang of guilt as she stood up. "I just have to help my dad with something."

"Gotcha."

She couldn't tell if he believed her. She didn't want to hurt his feelings, of course. But Tressa and the others could go zooming past at any moment. She had to get out of there.

"Well, nice to, uh, meet you," she said.

Was that too encouraging? She didn't want him to come over to her all the time. Tressa had said she should just ignore him and he'd go away. She needed to do that.

"Yeah, not a lot of anime nerds in Port Jeff," he said.

She almost responded but caught herself. If she started agreeing with him, they'd probably keep talking. And then she'd be stuck out in the open with Joel Applebaum for anyone to see. So she just gave him a tight smile and started walking back up the dock toward her house.

"Hey, I wanted to ask you something," he called after her.

She kept walking.

"What's it like to live in a haunted house?"

She froze. There were lots of things she could ignore. That wasn't one of them.

"What are you talking about?"

"You didn't know?" he asked. "Back in the 1930s, the boy who lived in your house died."

"You're making that up." She really hoped he was making it up.

He shrugged. "It's a local legend. For the last, like, eighty years, your house has mostly been empty. It's prime real estate or whatever, so every once in a while, someone buys it. But within a month or two, something always happens."

Morgan didn't want to know. She didn't want to ask. But she couldn't help herself.

"What happens?"

"Sometimes they just move out," said Joel. "Sometimes there's an accident."

FIVE

Morgan tried to tell herself that Joel was just trolling her. He probably sensed she was lying about having to help her dad and said her house was haunted to get back at her. That seemed the most likely answer.

But she couldn't get it out of her head the rest of the day. What if it was true? What if the boy had died in their living room, right where she liked to curl up on the couch and read? Or worse, what if he had died in her *bedroom*? How had he died? Had it been a terrible accident? Or *murder*?

Not even the Night Queen could distract her. Morgan

would start reading, and then there would be some sound, just a creak or a cough from her father's studio, and she would realize she'd stopped seeing the words on the page and was only thinking about how someone might have died in her house.

She logged on to the Night Queen chat server, thinking she'd ask people what they thought about it. Even if they just joked about it, maybe she'd feel better. But then she saw that Madison had posted some stupid meme about Tsuki the Moon Swordsman, who becomes Kosuke's rival for Zophia's affection in later volumes. It was the only thing she and Madison had ever argued about. As far as Morgan was concerned, Tsuki was boring and fussy, and Kosuke was the only possible choice for the Night Queen.

Seeing Madison argue with some *other* girl online about Tsuki vs. Kosuke made Morgan feel terrible—like she'd been totally replaced. So she closed the app without posting anything.

She was still fretting about ghosts that night at dinner. Unlike their old Brooklyn apartment, the new house was large enough to have a full kitchen and a dining room. For some reason, her parents had been really excited about that. Morgan would have been happy if they still sat on the couch and ate takeout every night like they used to. But now they had to "eat home-cooked meals at a real table like civilized folks," as her father put it.

Unfortunately neither of her parents were good cooks. Morgan looked down at the pile of mushy rice, soggy veggies, and rubbery tofu, and sighed. What she wouldn't give for a carton of Mr. Zhao's lo mein . . .

"What's up, sweetheart?" asked her mother.

"Oh, uh, nothing."

"You didn't stay down at the dock too long today," her father said.

"Yeah, I guess."

He grinned. "Harbor not majestic enough for you?"

"No, there was a boy there."

"A boy?" her mother asked sharply. "Was he mean to you?"

"Maybe? I don't know," said Morgan. "He said our house was haunted."

Her father's expression brightened. "Oh, that's right.

I remember the Realtor saying something about—*ouch!*" He gave Morgan's mother a guilty look. "I mean . . . haunted houses? How silly!"

Morgan glared at him. "I know Mom just kicked you under the table. You knew about it? Why didn't you tell me?"

"Sorry, sweetheart," said her mother. "We didn't want you to worry."

"So our house *is* haunted?"

"How else do you think we could afford a place like this?" asked her father.

Morgan's mom glared at him. "You are not helping." Then she turned back to Morgan. "No, of course our house is not haunted. Because there's no such thing as ghosts."

"Weeell . . ." Her father tilted his head, his face contemplative. "Ghosts could be considered symbols of lingering regrets, past injustices, or perhaps even echoes of past selves."

Morgan's mom closed her eyes and massaged the bridge of her nose with her thumb and forefinger. "Gabe, can we not get into a metaphysical discussion about ghosts right now?"

"Right, sorry." He turned to Morgan. "Honey, there's no such thing as real ghosts. I wish there were, but sadly, no."

Morgan stared at her father. "Why do you wish ghosts were *real*?"

His eyes lit up. "Are you kidding? Proof of an afterlife? The ability to directly contact and understand the past on a deeply human level? It would be *amazing*! Just think how—*ouch!*"

He glanced at Morgan's mother again.

"Sorry . . ."

"All I want to know," said Morgan, "is whether someone died in our house."

"It really doesn't matter, Morgan," said her mother. "The boy you met today was clearly trying to upset you. Don't let him."

That was easy for *her* to say. Morgan's mother was always so calm and thoughtful. Nothing ever rattled her. Morgan was more emotional and excitable like her father. But of course her mother was right. Ghosts didn't exist. Joel was just trolling her.

"I'll try," she promised.

And she did try. She and her parents made popcorn and watched a movie, and by the time she was getting into bed, she'd put all thoughts of ghosts out of her mind.

She was on volume three of *My Secret Dream of a Boring Life*. This was the volume where the story got more serious. At the end of volume two, Zophia revealed that she was not human, and she was relieved that Kosuke and the others still accepted her.

Zophia did not, however, tell them that she was the dread Night Queen who had conquered their realm. That didn't happen until volume three, when one of her generals, Tsuki the Moon Swordsman, showed up with terrible news. While she was fooling around with humans, two of her other generals, Dym the Earthen Wizard and Piorun the Mysl Grandmaster, had conspired together and were now trying to seize the throne for themselves. Zophia had to make a choice. She could leave behind this new life she'd made with Kosuke and the other humans to defend her throne, or she could remain happily where she was and let the generals take the kingdom.

But of course it wasn't that simple. Zophia knew that if Dym and Piorun took power, they'd want to enslave all the humans, including Kosuke and the other friends she'd made. So she decided to give up her beautiful boring life so that she could protect the people she cared about. That meant it was time for war, and for the true power of the Night Queen to emerge . . .

TAP

"Absolutely not."

Morgan quickly leaned over and slammed the window shut.

That obnoxious dripping would not work on her this time. And what about the crying she'd heard last night? She'd half convinced herself she'd imagined it, but what if it had been Joel that whole time, laying the groundwork for his ghost trolling? The dripping had been one thing, but how else could she explain the crying? Joel had *seemed* like a nice guy, but the girls had called him a creepy weirdo. Maybe it was because he was one of those horrible boys who enjoyed pranking people. What if he'd been sitting outside her window the last few nights messing with her and laughing to himself?

The idea made her so mad that she couldn't get to sleep. After tossing and turning for a while, she gave up and decided a late-night snack might soothe her.

But when she got down to the kitchen, nothing was really calling out to her. She stared into the open fridge, trying to decide if there was anything that might make her feel better. Cheese stick? Orange? None of it grabbed her.

TAP

The hairs on the back of her neck rose. The kitchen suddenly felt colder than any open fridge could make it.

TAP

She slowly turned and saw the kitchen faucet dripping. It had never done that before.

TAP

But that wasn't so crazy, right? Faucets dripped. Of course they did. Someone probably hadn't completely shut it off. Maybe even her. She'd been pretty distracted when she'd been rinsing the dishes after dinner.

TAP

She stepped over and yanked hard on the handle.

TAP

It didn't work.

She jiggled it, thinking that might fix it somehow. Instead a big spurt of water came out. But it wasn't regular sink water. It was dark and cloudy, and there was a thread of slimy green seaweed in it. As if it was . . .

"Seawater," she whispered.

She watched it swirl down the drain. Once it was gone, she reached out to turn the faucet on again, but hesitated. What if it was more seawater? What did that mean? How was it even possible?

"You still up, honey?"

Her dad stood behind her, holding the empty popcorn bowl from earlier.

"Uh, yeah," she said.

He gave her a quizzical look.

"You okay?"

"Sure."

She stepped away and watched intently as he rinsed out the bowl. This time it was totally normal, clear sink water. And when he turned it off, it stayed off. No drip. Everything was fine.

So why didn't she feel better?

CHAPTER

SIX

Seawater coming out of a faucet did not prove the existence of ghosts. Morgan knew that. But the ocean followed her into dreams. That night she woke up three times from a nightmare about drowning. Each time, she came awake gasping, her lungs burning as though she'd been holding her breath while she was asleep.

The next day, Sunday, Morgan's father was still on deadline, but her mother didn't have to go into the city for work, so she decided it was time to finally finish unpacking. With Morgan's help, of course.

They'd been in the house for over a month, and all

the essentials had been put in their proper places. But there was holiday stuff, old paper files, and little decorative knickknacks all still in boxes.

They took care of the knickknacks first. These were little things like framed pictures and tchotchkes that needed to be placed strategically on bookshelves and hung on walls. Even though Morgan's father didn't draw superhero comics, he still loved them, so there were a lot of collectibles that needed homes. Morgan's mom had a weird thing for foxes, so there were lots of fox figurines that needed to be placed too. And with this big house, there were so many more options. Sadly there were no Night Queen decorations because it wasn't mainstream enough yet for toys or models. Maybe once the anime came out, there would be some.

Thinking of the anime made Morgan think of Joel, which then made her mad. It sucked that the first anime fan she'd found on Long Island was a creepy weirdo. Well, she wouldn't let him spoil it, or *anything* for that matter. In fact, now that she'd placed her father's prized Sandman figure on the mantel and her mother's nine-tailed fox statue in the stairwell, this place was starting to feel less like some spooky haunted house and more like her home. So it had some weird plumbing issues. Nowhere was perfect.

Sadly the fun unpacking was over pretty quickly. Then there was just the stuff that needed to be crammed into the attic crawl space. And since it was so cramped, it was Morgan's job to climb up there and organize it all. This was the not-fun part.

The crawl space was accessed from a narrow, rickety ladder that dropped down from the ceiling in the upstairs hallway. There were no lights or windows up there. It wasn't insulated, so bits of sunlight shone through cracks in the roof, but she still needed a flashlight. It was hot and stuffy and so dusty that she could feel her throat drying out with each breath.

The ceiling in the crawl space was high enough for her to sit up, but not to stand. Her mother shoved boxes up one at a time, and Morgan slid them around, trying to find the best way to fit everything while keeping it all more or less organized. And of course she had to maintain a central aisle so she would be able to reach the stuff in the back at some point in the future.

It didn't take all that long, but she was sweaty, gross, and miserable by the end. Morgan's eyes itched from the dust, and she'd torn her sock on a nail that stuck out of the rough floorboards. Then, worst of all, just as she shoved the last box into place, she got a splinter in her knee.

It wasn't in too deep. She was able to get most of it out with her fingers, but it still hurt. She glared at the offending board that dared injure her and noticed it was a slightly different color from the rest. In fact, when she focused the flashlight and looked closer, she saw that it seemed to be loose.

Careful not to get any more splinters, she lifted it up, and was surprised and delighted to find a hidden space underneath. A *secret* space. And inside was an ancient-looking leather satchel.

Was this possibly the coolest thing that had ever happened to her? Maybe so. What was in the satchel? A treasure map? A lost work of art or manuscript? Maybe just a bunch of really old money?

Anything seemed plausible and she was ready for it.

She carefully lifted the satchel and placed it on her lap. She brushed away the thick layer of dust, then opened it up. Inside were two things: an old, yellowed newspaper clipping and a child-sized uniform.

The newspaper clipping was dated August 1, 1937. The headline read:

LOCAL BOY BELIEVED DROWNED

At approximately eight o'clock in the morning, the remains of a small sailboat washed ashore in East Setauket. The vessel originated at Port Jefferson and after an extensive investigation, police determined that it was likely stolen by twelve-year-old Joseph Klaus, who had run away from his summer camp in Yaphank two days before. Authorities believe he may have been trying to reach his home on the other side of the harbor, but was caught in the recent storm and drowned. No body has been recovered.

There was more to the article, but that was all Morgan needed to read. This was the boy Joel had been talking about. The boy who died. The story was heartbreaking and distressing, but at least he hadn't died *in* the house. That was something.

Next she examined the child-sized uniform.

There was a tan button-down shirt, dark shorts . . .

And a red armband with a Nazi swastika.

SEVEN

Morgan stared down at the Nazi swastika for a long time. Long enough for her mother to call up to her in a concerned voice. Rather than reply immediately, Morgan tucked the newspaper clipping and the uniform under her arm, and climbed down the ladder.

She held them out to her mother and said in a quiet voice, "I found these."

Morgan's mother was normally so calm and collected, but when she saw the Nazi swastika, she gasped and physically recoiled from it. After a moment, she composed herself and took the bundle from Morgan.

"Sweetie, let's have a chat."

A few minutes later, they were sitting at the kitchen table, Morgan with her seltzer, and her mom with a cup of chai. Morgan didn't like chai, but she did like how it smelled. The distinct blend of cardamom, cinnamon, and ginger that drifted up from her mother's I'M THE BOSS mug reminded her of the cozy comfort of their old Brooklyn apartment.

"Morgan," her mother said. "You know that the Nazis weren't just villains in a Captain America movie, right? They were real."

"I know that," said Morgan. "The Nazis were the bad guys we fought in World War Two."

"And you know the Nazis did more than just try to conquer Europe. They also tried to exterminate all the Jewish people in the world, as well as gay people and Roma people."

"The Holocaust, right? We learned about that in school. But the Nazis were in Germany. So why is there a Nazi uniform *here*?"

"I'm sad to say, there were some Americans who agreed with the Nazis."

"How is that even possible?" asked Morgan.

"I don't know," her mom admitted. "Even now, there are people who try to claim that the Nazis weren't as bad as everyone made them out to be, and that the Holocaust wasn't real."

"But don't we have pictures of it all?"

"We have *lots* of evidence," said her mother. "Photographs, film, documents, personal testimony from victims, and even confessions from former Nazis."

"So how can people say it wasn't true?" asked Morgan.

"I wish I knew," said her mother.

Morgan looked down at the folded uniform that lay on the table between them. Some kid back in the 1930s had worn this. Had that kid really wanted all those people to be killed?

"What do we do with it?" she asked.

"I'm going to see if there's a local museum or historical society that wants it," said her mother.

"You think it should be in a museum exhibit?" asked Morgan.

Her mother's brown eyes were piercing. "Humanity

can never forget what the Nazis did, and we can never let it happen again."

Morgan felt uneasy the rest of the day, and that night decided to read in the living room rather than her bedroom. Just in case there would be more dripping and crying. Not that she really thought she was being haunted by a ghost Nazi boy or anything . . .

But once she went to bed, Morgan's dreams were filled with Nazi soldiers. They chased her across a never-ending field. Then suddenly the ground beneath her vanished and she plunged into a deep ocean. Her arms and legs flailed helplessly as she tried to swim back to the surface, which was always just out of reach. Her lungs burned for air. She had to clamp down on the impulse to breathe, knowing she would only suck in the dark water that surrounded her. That was the scariest part of drowning—feeling your chest heave with the urge to breathe, even when you *knew* there was nothing but the cold vastness of the ocean all around you . . .

Morgan snapped awake, shivering and drenched in sweat. It was very early morning, still pretty dark.

She sat up in bed, feeling disoriented. The dream had seemed so real.

Then she felt something strange in her mouth. She fished around with her fingers until she pulled a slimy tendril of seaweed from between her lips.

She stared at the wet green strand uncomprehendingly as it dangled between her thumb and forefinger. Then she recalled the headline of that old newspaper clipping:

LOCAL BOY BELIEVED DROWNED

She rinsed her mouth out repeatedly with mouthwash. But afterward she thought she could still faintly taste the grit of seawater.

CHAPTER EIGHT

Zophia Zye, who came to be known as the Night Queen, didn't start off as royalty. In fact, she and her family were peasants who lived in a rural oni village where people didn't know how to read. When soldiers posted a sign warning the villagers that they needed to evacuate because of an imminent volcano eruption, none of them even realized they were in danger until it was too late. Zophia was the only person in the whole village who survived, and that was because her parents sacrificed themselves to get her to safety.

After Zophia realized what had happened—how *easy* it would have been to prevent the tragedy, if only they'd known—she sat down at a crossroads and wept. Then a mysterious being appeared and asked why she was crying. When she told him her sad story, he felt bad for her. He revealed that he was a god and said he would grant her one wish. She wished for the ability to read anything, in any language, no matter what, so she would never suffer the same terrible ignorance again.

When the mysterious god granted her wish, it was like Zophia saw the world in a completely new way. Some of it was good, and some of it was bad.

Morgan felt similarly, except it was pretty much all bad. The world around her, which only yesterday had seemed safe and normal, now felt like a darker, more dangerous place. Nazis in Long Island? It just didn't make sense. Yet clearly it had been true, and according to her mother, it might even *still* be true. It was also getting harder and harder to convince herself that Joel had made up the idea that her house was haunted. In fact, it might be even worse than he'd said. It wasn't merely a ghost—it was a *Nazi* ghost.

She was once more tempted to hide in her corner during lunch, but forced herself to sit with Hannah, Tressa, and Piper again. It was actually a little easier. Maybe because she really didn't want to be alone.

The girls were talking about what a great time they'd had wakeboarding, and how Jake had totally been flirting with Piper the whole time. Morgan was barely paying attention though. She just stared at them and wondered if any of their families had been Nazis.

"How long have your families lived here?" she asked abruptly.

They all seemed a little thrown off by her question, which she supposed was understandable.

"Why?" asked Tressa.

"Oh, uh . . ." Morgan decided that straight up asking them if their ancestors had been Nazis was not a great way to make friends. "Just curious. You all seem like you've known each other forever."

"The three of us basically grew up together," said Tressa. "My parents moved here from Jersey when I was a baby."

"What about you two?" Morgan asked, trying to

make the question seem more casual than it actually felt. "Did your parents move here when you were babies?"

"Hmm." Piper's pale face frowned. "No, my parents grew up here too. I think it was my grandparents who moved here from Ohio. I still have relatives in Cleveland, but we don't see them very much."

"Ha, I have you both beat," said Hannah, ever competitive. "I know for a fact that my *great*-grandpa moved here when he was little, like, forever ago."

Morgan tried to think about her own great-grandparents. The last one had died when she was only five so she didn't really remember them. But her parents and grandparents talked about them, and she was pretty sure at least one of her great-grandfathers had been in World War II. That meant Hannah's family had probably been in Port Jefferson back when Joseph Klaus drowned. And Hannah's last name was Meyer, which Morgan was pretty sure was German. In theory, they *could* have been Nazis . . .

"Whoa, what's up, new girl?" asked Tressa. "You look like you just saw a ghost."

Morgan laughed nervously. "Yeah. I mean, supposedly I live in a haunted house, so . . ." She shrugged, trying to play it off.

But all three of them looked at her with wide eyes.

"Wait, that's *you?*" asked Tressa.

"Oh, wow, that's super scary," Piper said sympathetically.

"So not only do you live down the street from a creepy weirdo, you also live in the neighborhood haunted house?" asked Hannah. "You really lucked out, new girl."

Morgan felt her heart sink. There went her last shred of hope that Joel had made it all up. "You've . . . all heard about it?"

"Of *course,*" said Tressa. "Anybody who grew up around here can tell you about the haunted house."

"Yeah, Tress, you remember when we were little kids?" asked Hannah. "We would hold our breath when we walked past the house because we were afraid the ghost would possess us or something."

"R-Really?" asked Morgan.

"I heard somebody finally moved in, but I didn't

realize that was *you*." Tressa looked truly concerned. "Wow ..."

"Seriously," said Hannah.

"Stop it, you guys," said Piper. "You're really freaking her out."

"Nah," lied Morgan, trying desperately to act cool. "It's not like I really believe in, like, ghost Nazis or anything."

"Ghost *what* now?" asked Tressa.

All three looked confused. Why had Morgan brought up the Nazi part?

"The boy who died ..." she mumbled awkwardly. "He was like a Nazi or something ..."

Hannah's eyes narrowed. "And you know this because ..."

"Well, I found this ..." But now they were looking at her like *she* was the creepy weirdo. "N-Never mind. It's dumb."

"*Anyway*," said Hannah, making it clear they were done with the topic. "I asked my mom about going into the city next weekend, and you know what she said?"

The other girls seemed eager to shift focus, and as

they chattered on about whatever, Morgan felt like they were more or less ignoring her now. Why did she have to go babbling about ghost Nazis, even if it *was* true? Port Jeff Middle was a small school, and there weren't a lot of friend options.

Had she just blown her only real chance?

CHAPTER

NINE

There were, Morgan decided, levels of loneliness. She thought she'd felt pretty lonely when she first moved to Long Island and couldn't hang out with Madison anymore. But then she'd felt lonelier when she began school and realized that making new friends would not be as easy as she'd hoped.

Now she felt even lonelier. Not because she had even fewer friends. That was impossible because you couldn't have negative friends. But she felt the loneliness more deeply because she had this . . . *thing* that she couldn't talk about with anyone.

Well, that wasn't exactly true. There was one person she could probably talk to about it. She just wasn't sure she wanted to.

The way home from school took her through a commercial district along the harbor. There were some clothing stores, a cute little pet supply store, and a lot of restaurants. Some seemed really modern, and some seemed like they'd been there forever. One of the oldest was an ice-cream parlor. Morgan had taken note of it on her first week because it was the only place in town she could get a proper egg cream, which her father had taught her at an early age was an important thing to know.

Morgan had a little bit of money on her, and as she neared the ice-cream shop, she thought about treating herself to an egg cream, or maybe even an ice-cream float. It has been a stressful couple days and she deserved a treat.

Except Joel Applebaum was in there. She could see him through the window, sitting on one of the stools at the long, old-fashioned counter. She supposed she could go in there, order an egg cream, and just ignore him.

But with all these thoughts of ghost Nazis floating around in her brain, she didn't know if she could resist bringing it up to the one person who seemed willing to talk about "creepy" things. And that presented a huge risk. If she *did* talk to him, she would also be in clear view of the front window. Any neighborhood kids who walked by would see her hanging out with the creepy weirdo. In fact, it was even more likely she would be spotted here than when they'd been talking on the dock.

She decided an egg cream wasn't worth the risk, and kept walking.

Once she was out of the downtown area, the street gradually sloped upward, and fancy old homes lined both sides. Her mom said they were "Victorian style." Morgan loved how bright and colorful they were. One was sky blue and dark pink; another was lemon yellow and hunter green. Each one was unique, with large porches that looked out over the harbor below. They were so different from the uniform brownstones she'd grown up with in Brooklyn. She loved those too, of course, but she felt like these houses were something special.

Eventually the street flattened out, then sloped back down. Near the bottom of the hill was the turn into the little cul-de-sac where she lived. The houses there weren't as fancy as the Victorian-style homes, but they were all two stories with a small garage, and a little balcony that looked out at the water across the street.

She had a nice house in a nice place. She should appreciate it. But when she turned to look out at the harbor that sparkled golden in the afternoon sun, she remembered the boy who had drowned. A sudden chill went through her. Instead of admiring the view, she hurried inside.

Morgan didn't say much at dinner, but her parents didn't notice. Her father had made his deadline, and her mother had closed on some big contract, so they were both feeling pretty good about themselves and spent the evening congratulating each other.

After dinner, she went back to her room, intent on completely submerging herself in the second half of volume three of *My Secret Dream of a Boring Life*, which was all about titanic battles between Zophia Zye and her two former generals.

"You disappoint me, General Piorun," I told the Mysl Grandmaster as we faced off on the ruined parapets of my palace. "I had thought the elves shared my vision for a united continent."

"United, yes!" said the wily old elf. His hands worked feverishly to shape a spell that he clearly hoped, against all evidence to the contrary, would prevent my retribution. "But this new-found fondness of yours for humans is an abomination!"

"The only abomination I see," I told him, "is an elf who seeks to destroy anyone different from himself. Now prepare to face my wrath!"

"Ugh!"

Morgan was startled out of the story by her mother's yelp of alarm from down the hall.

"Mom?" she called worriedly. "You okay?"

"Yeah, I'm fine." Her mother sounded more irritated than anything. "Gabe! Something's wrong with the plumbing!"

Morgan felt a tremor of unease, thinking of what had happened to the kitchen sink. "What's wrong with the plumbing?"

"The bathwater looks *disgusting*." Her mother stepped into Morgan's doorway wearing a bathrobe, her expression sour. "I was really looking forward to a nice long bath . . ."

Morgan put her book down, her dread growing. It was probably nothing. Coincidence. But she couldn't help asking, "Disgusting *how*?"

"See for yourself." Her mother trudged disappointedly back to her own bedroom.

Morgan didn't hurry to the bathroom, mostly because she was afraid of what she would find. And she was right.

The bathtub was filled with seawater and thin ribbons of seaweed.

"Whoa, that's weird," said her father as he peered over Morgan's shoulder.

"Yeah . . ."

The sight of the seaweed floating in that grimy water sent a wave of nausea through her. She walked numbly back to her room, wondering what it all meant, and fearing she already knew.

She glanced over to the window. Since the weather had gotten cooler, she hadn't opened it that night. Now she walked over and yanked it up.

It was that same crying as before—a heartbroken sob that simultaneously wrenched at her heart and made her want to crawl out of her skin. But it was louder this time. More insistent. In fact, her father could hear it from the bathroom.

"Yikes, what *is* that?" he called.

"Dad, come here!"

She heard his heavy tread down the hallway toward her. But just as he stepped into her room, the weeping stopped.

"What is it, honey?" he asked.

"Did you hear that?" she demanded. "That *crying*?"

He nodded. "Of course. It was probably a cat."

"A *cat*?" How could he think that sounded like a cat?

He shrugged. "What else would it be?"

She wanted to shout at him, *IT'S A GHOST NAZI!!!* But she knew he didn't believe in ghosts. Or he did,

but only in some confusing metaphysical way...
Regardless, she wouldn't be able to convince him.
Instead he'd be concerned that she was imagining
things, because she was a lonely loser who had no
friends and spent all her time in her bedroom reading
silly Japanese fantasy stories.

So she reined in her emotions and forced a smile
onto her lips.

"Yeah." She slid the window shut. "A cat. That's all
it was."

CHAPTER

TEN

Morgan had promised to try harder to make friends, but the next day she just couldn't muster up the determination, especially after rambling to Tressa and the others about ghost Nazis the day before. So at lunch period, she sat by herself and retreated into the familiar comforting world of the Night Queen.

After school, she passed the ice-cream parlor on her way home and saw Joel once again sitting at the counter. This time, she didn't hurry past. Instead she looked more closely. He was reading the light novel for volume one of *My Secret Dream of a Boring Life*.

That was strange. He'd already read the manga, so it wasn't like he needed to read the novel version. Was he reading it because *she* had recommended it?

A surge of warmth in her chest made her feel a little less alone. She couldn't quite put it into words, but she found she wanted to answer the question he'd asked on Saturday. What was it like to live in a haunted house? She was pretty sure she knew.

She pulled open the door, walked into the ice-cream parlor, and sat down next to him. He didn't notice at first because he was reading so intently. It reminded Morgan of how often her mom complained about *her* being the same way. Sometimes her mother would have to call up several times before Morgan heard her.

Once Joel finished the chapter, he closed the book, then his dark eyebrows jumped up on his pale forehead.

"Oh, hey," he said.

"What do you think?" She nodded to the book.

He could have said something easy like "It was great" or even "okay." Instead he frowned thoughtfully for a moment, then said, "She's a lot sadder than I realized."

"Sad?"

"Yeah, it's not as obvious in the manga. But with the light novel, you really do get inside her head, and you realize that even though she's surrounded by all these generals and loyal soldiers—even Zsa Zsa—she's actually pretty lonely. None of them really see the girl *behind* the Night Queen. Do you know what I mean?"

"Yeah." The warm glow in her chest grew stronger. Joel *got it.* He really did. Maybe even better than Madison.

There was an awkward moment of silence.

"You asked me what it was like to live in a haunted house," she said.

"Oh." He looked embarrassed. "Sorry. I shouldn't have—"

"It's *horrible.*" Her throat tightened up and suddenly she was fighting back tears. All the stress and fear rushed to the surface, like finally talking about it had unlocked a floodgate that she could now barely hold shut.

He stared at her.

Her chest tightened when she realized that maybe it

had been a joke. Maybe she had completely misjudged him and he was going to laugh at her now.

But he didn't laugh. Instead he asked, "Are you okay?"

"I don't know." Her voice warbled, and the suppressed tears stung her eyes. She took a deep breath before continuing. "I found . . . a Nazi uniform in the attic."

His eyes widened. *"Nazis?"*

"A *kid* Nazi uniform. And there was an old newspaper article about a boy named Joseph Klaus who drowned in the harbor."

"Wait, he didn't die in the house?"

Morgan shook her head. "The newspaper said he was running away from his summer camp for some reason? And he stole a boat, then tried to sail across the harbor to get home."

"To your house."

"Yeah."

They looked at each other.

"So . . ." Joel hesitated for a moment. "Have you experienced any, like, *ghost* things?"

Morgan told him about the dripping and the crying, the seaweed and seawater. As she was talking, Joel's eyes kept getting bigger. By the time she was done, he looked as scared as she felt.

They sat in silence for a moment, but now it was more tense than awkward. Morgan watched Joel anxiously as he thought about it, his brow furrowed, his eyes fixed somewhere unseen.

"I don't think your house is haunted," he said at last.

She wanted to feel relieved, but the pinched expression on his face didn't give her the impression that she should.

"No?" she pressed.

"I'm no expert, of course. But I think in order for a house to be haunted, the person has to die *inside* it."

"Then what do you think is going on? Do you think I'm . . . *imagining* it?"

He shook his head. "I think this boy, Joseph Klaus, is still trying to get home."

Something cold and dark filled her stomach.

"You think a ghost is trying to get into my house?"

He nodded. "Any way it can."

"And . . . what happens if it does?"

"You remember what I said before about accidents?

The last one happened ten years ago. I read about it. Apparently the mom slipped and broke her neck in the bathroom."

"Is that a thing that happens?" Morgan had never thought of the bathroom of all places as dangerous.

"That's what I wondered, so I looked it up. I guess like six thousand people a year in the US die from falling in their home," said Joel. "But this gets weirder. The woman slipped because the bathroom was flooded. With *seawater*. And they could never explain how that happened."

"Seawater . . ." The memory of her bathtub filled with seawater came back, bringing with it a swirl of fear and nausea. What if it had spilled over and her mother had slipped on it? *She* could have broken her neck . . .

"I'm worried that the ghost is going to keep trying to get in." Joel broke into her thoughts. "And things are just going to get worse until something really bad happens."

She stared at him, trying—and failing—to rid her mind of the image of her mom, neck broken, lying on the bathroom floor.

"Wh-what do I do?"

"I don't know." He leaned toward her, looking intent. "But . . . can I help?"

She laughed out loud with relief, her eyes stinging once more. "Yeah. That would be great."

CHAPTER ELEVEN

Morgan and Joel walked most of the way home together, but they spoke little. Morgan felt like there was so much going on in her head, she didn't know what to say. On one hand, the idea of a ghost invading her home was terrifying. On the other, it was such a relief to feel like she didn't have to deal with it alone anymore. Those girls got Joel all wrong. Maybe he used to be a creepy weirdo when they were all growing up together. But there was nothing creepy or weird about him now. He was a genuinely nice guy.

They reached Joel's house first.

"I'm going to research Joseph Klaus," he promised.

"Thanks," she said.

She watched him walk up his drive and let himself into his house. It was getting dark, and she was now keenly aware that she was alone. It was only half a block from Joel's house to hers, but it felt like a very long half block. As she walked, she wondered if the ghost ever appeared, or if it was only sounds and water. If it *did* appear, what would it look like? The boy had drowned, so he would probably be dripping and festooned with seaweed, gray and bloated, empty eye sockets and purple lips, skin half-eaten by crabs . . .

She shuddered. The problem with having an active imagination was that it often took her to places she did not want to go.

Finally she reached her house, which, at least for now, was safe. If the ghost was trying to get inside, that meant it wasn't actually inside *yet*. Right? She really hoped that was what it meant.

Just like the sink, the bathtub had gone back to providing clean tap water on its own. Now it seemed like her parents had completely forgotten it even happened. When she asked her father, he'd dismissed it.

"Probably just some sort of temporary underground plumbing issue. We do live right next to the ocean, after all." Then he grinned at her. "I mean the *harbor*, of course."

She mustered a smile of appreciation for the callback, but it was a little forced.

After enduring another soggy tofu dinner, Morgan retired to her bedroom for some soothing Night Queen. Volume four was a big shift in the story, and a lot more fun. After reclaiming her throne, Zophia Zye tried to better integrate her human and nonhuman subjects so that humans, elves, dwarves, trolls, and oni all worked together harmoniously, making sure that Kosuke and her other human friends had a place at her court. A lot of the conflicts in volume four came down to silly cultural misunderstandings that she had to resolve between the humans and nonhumans. It was a nice break, both from the battles of volume three and Morgan's real-life fears of an invading ghost.

"Morgan."

Her father stood in the doorway. His eyes were so large and round, he looked like *he'd* just seen a ghost.

She sat up, her pulse racing. "Dad, are you okay?"

"Morgan," he said again, his tone unsure, as if he could hardly believe what he was saying. "There is a boy at the front door who would like to speak with you. A handsome, well-spoken boy. I am not ready for this. Can I tell him to go away until I've had time to process the idea that my daughter is growing up?"

She sighed with relief. "Only if you're striving for the worst parent in the world award."

"Hmm, tempting . . ." His expression abruptly relaxed. "But it sounds like a lot of paperwork. I guess you should talk to him."

Morgan went downstairs and saw Joel standing on the other side of the screen door.

"Did you find something already?"

"Yeah." He held up his laptop. "Can I come in? You're going to want to see this."

As soon as she let him in, her parents suddenly appeared, which meant they had already been lurking. Morgan supposed she couldn't blame them. This was the first time a boy had come over. They probably had all kinds of wrong assumptions.

"Who's your friend, Morgan?" asked her mom.

"Uh, this is Joel," she said.

"Joel Applebaum," he told her parents. "I live a few doors down. It's nice to meet you both."

"See what I mean?" Morgan's father whispered loudly to her mother. "So well-spoken!"

Morgan ignored that. "We're working on a project for school together."

"Right," said Joel. "A, uh, history project."

"Hmmm . . ." Her dad gazed at Joel, clearly trying to look intimidating, and just as clearly failing. "I *suppose* that's okay."

"*If* you work in the living room," her mom said firmly.

"Okay, okay. Come on, Joel." Morgan motioned for him to follow her into the living room. "But no spying, you two."

"Spying?" her father asked her mother, looking somewhere between hurt and offended. *"Us?"*

Her mother took him by the ear and led him toward the kitchen. "Come on, you."

Once her parents were out of earshot, she plopped down on the couch and looked at Joel.

"Okay, what did you figure out?"

He sat down beside her and opened his laptop. "I didn't figure out anything. All I did was search 'Long Island Nazi kids' and it was the top result."

He spun his laptop around for her to see.

"Camp Siegfried?" she asked, reading the article title.

"Apparently in the 1930s there was this group called the German American Bund. Basically they were a Hitler fan club in America before World War Two. They did all kinds of Nazi propaganda stuff, like opening a summer camp for kids in Yaphank."

"Yaphank?" Morgan asked sharply. "That's where the newspaper said Joseph Klaus's summer camp was."

"So he probably went to this Camp Siegfried," said Joel. "And check this place out."

He clicked through a couple of pictures, and all she could say was:

"This was in *America*?"

"About twelve miles from where we're sitting right now," he said grimly.

The black-and-white pictures really did look like something from a Captain America movie. One showed a line of stone-faced white men in Nazi uniforms. Another showed buildings with swastikas built into the brickwork. There was even a garden where some hedges had been shaped into a big swastika. And just in case anyone was still confused, there were signs for Goebbels Street, Goering Street, and of course Adolf Hitler Street.

"How was this even possible?" she asked.

"I guess since we weren't at war with them yet, it wasn't against the law." He pointed to another picture. "Anyway, this is the one that I think sheds some light on who our ghost was."

It was a scan of an old newspaper photo that showed orderly rows of children, all different ages, some of them no more than five or six years old. They were all in uniform, and all with their arms outstretched in the "Heil Hitler" salute. It was chilling in a way Morgan couldn't articulate.

"Joseph Klaus was one of these kids," she whispered.

"And something happened to him at that camp."

Joel leaned over and gazed at the picture with her. "Something so terrible that he escaped, somehow crossed twelve miles of land, stole a boat, and tried to sail across the harbor alone at night, in the middle of a storm, to get back home."

Joel looked at Morgan.

"To get back *here*."

INTERLUDE

The German phrase *Herzlich Willkommen* was emblazoned on a sign above the front gate of Camp Siegfried. Joseph Klaus didn't know what it meant when he first arrived, but later he learned that it meant "Hearty Welcome."

There were a lot of things Joseph didn't know when he first arrived at Camp Siegfried. But he learned quickly—because if he didn't, he was punished.

He learned that he could not speak English, only German. He learned that America had become corrupted by Jews, who were evil monsters disguised as people, and the only thing that could save the country was the Führer. He learned that to serve the Führer, he must become strong and tough. He could never cry or show any emotion. Even if he was exhausted after marching all night with a twenty-pound backpack. Even if the other boys teased him after they found out that his mother was Greek rather than German. Even if he accidentally smashed his finger while being forced to lay bricks all day in the hot sun for a new building. He had to prove that he was German enough, despite his "impure" blood. Otherwise, when the time came to rise up against the American government and the disease they called democracy, he would be left behind.

He *did* cry, of course. Every night when he collapsed onto his bedroll in the tent he shared with other boys, he pressed his face into his pillow to muffle his quiet sobs.

His parents had said this would be good for him. They said it would be challenging and that he needed to be brave and not complain.

Was this what they meant? It must be. They loved him, after all, and just wanted to make sure he had a place in the new Nazi order that would surely come.

CHAPTER

TWELVE

MorganLeZye: Anybody know if theres a way to deal with ghosts? You know how werewolves hate silver, and vampires hate garlic and sunlight. What do ghosts hate?

ZsaZsa-Stan-chan: Morgan where have you been???? I haven't seen you here in forever!!!

MorganLeZye: my family just moved so weve been busy

THEE_NightQueen_QUEEN: why do u want to know about ghosts?

A few nights before, Morgan had wanted to post about the ghost in the chat because she'd hoped someone would talk her out of believing in it. Now that she was convinced it was real, the last thing she wanted was someone arguing with her that it wasn't. Fortunately someone else came up with an alternate reason for her ghost question:

> **ZsaZsa-Stan-chan**: i bet she's writing NQ fanfic with ghosts in it!

> **THEE_NightQueen_QUEEN**: hm ya i guess they never did ghosts in the series

> **MorganLeZye**: that's the reason. So anyone know?

> **MadMadison**: for ghosts you burn sage in the house. if that doesn't get rid of them, you have to burn their remains.

Morgan hated that Madison was the one who had the answer.

> **THEE_NightQueen_QUEEN**: why u know so much about ghosts, maddy?

MadMadison: I just did a search. took
like 2 seconds

What Madison meant was that Morgan was being lazy and should have just searched for it herself instead of posting the question on the server.

MorganLeZye: k thx!

She really hoped the sarcasm in her gratitude got through, but knowing Madison, probably not.

And of course Madison was right. Morgan did a search and found all sorts of websites that talked about ghosts, poltergeists, possession, and other stuff. It was hard to tell which she could trust, but nearly all of them seemed to agree that "smudging," or burning dried sage in each room, was the place to start. Morgan wasn't sure if it would work, since smudging seemed to be about getting a ghost out of the house, rather than *keeping* it out, but she figured it couldn't hurt.

Of course, then she had to find some sage. It was a seasoning, right? Maybe now that her parents cooked, they had some in the kitchen.

She found a whole rack of spice jars in the pantry, and fortunately one of them was labeled SAGE.

The next question was how she should burn it. It looked like crumbled dry leaves, so it would probably burn pretty easily. But how would she do it without setting anything else on fire?

After some thought, she took out a small ceramic bowl and poured the sage into it. That was how priests burned incense, after all, so it was probably the same thing. Then she found a box of matches in a drawer and lit one.

She hesitated for a moment, holding the burning match over the sage. Was this really a good idea?

Well, she had to do *something*, didn't she? Besides, the match was burning down and she was beginning to feel the heat on the tips of her finger and thumb.

She let the match drop into the bowl.

A ball of fire erupted, shooting up so high that Morgan yelped and leaped back. But the fire was quickly hidden in a thick, pungent cloud of smoke. It wasn't a *bad* smell, exactly, but it still made her cough. She waved her hand back and forth to clear the smoke as she tried to look into the bowl.

There was nothing except a tiny bit of ash now. The whole thing had burned up all at once.

Morgan sighed, which was a mistake because then she breathed in more of the sage smoke, which made her cough even more.

She wasn't sure what she'd done wrong, but it looked like the only room that was getting "smudged" was the kitchen. At least that meant there wouldn't be any more seawater coming out of the sink.

Hopefully.

Assuming any of this worked.

"Morgan?"

She wheeled around to see her father in the kitchen doorway. His eyes narrowed.

"Were you trying to cook something?" he asked.

"Oh, uh . . ." Morgan had never been very good at lying, especially to her father, so she didn't even try. "No, I was trying to do something called smudging, but I don't think I did it right."

"Smudging?" He looked no less confused. "Like with a stick of sage?"

"It comes in sticks?" she asked.

His eyes moved to the empty glass seasoning jar. "You thought sage was like incense or something?"

"Except it's not," she said.

"Definitely not. But why did you want to smudge the house?"

"So you know about smudging?"

"Sure. To get rid of evil spirits, bad vibes, and stuff like that . . ." Then he tilted his head back and closed his eyes as understanding dawned. "Oh! I get it. You're still freaked out about the house being haunted?"

"I'm not freaked out," she protested, even though she definitely was.

"Worried, then," he amended. "What if I took you to a shop that sells sage bundles that are made specifically for smudging?"

Her eyes widened. "Will you?"

"If you're going to keep lighting things on fire, I'd rather it be properly done and under adult supervision." He added, "And you're paying for it. It'll only be a couple bucks, so it shouldn't hurt your book budget too badly."

"I'll go get my money."

"You want to go right now?" he asked.

"Of course."

Morgan made her way upstairs to her bedroom and grabbed the small wad of cash she kept in an old Pokémon card tin on her dresser. On her way back downstairs, she walked past the glass doors to the balcony, and noticed a blond boy crouched on the railing.

She froze.

Blond boy?

Her heart thundered in her chest as she turned slowly—almost unwillingly—back toward the glass doors.

The railing was empty.

Of *course* it was. Because how on earth could a boy be perched on a second-floor balcony?

Although wait, no, it wasn't completely empty. Something dark and thin dangled from the rail. Like strips of seaweed.

No, it had to be something else.

She closed her eyes and took a deep breath, partly to calm down, partly to quell the nausea that now seemed to come whenever she saw seaweed, and partly because she hoped whatever it was would also disappear. But when she opened her eyes, the dark tendrils were still there. So after another moment, she reluctantly slid the door open and stepped through.

The balcony was small—just big enough for a few chairs and a tiny table that could hold some snacks or a couple of drinking glasses. Once she was out there, she saw that indeed a few ribbons of seaweed dangled from the railing.

"Morgan, honey? You ready?" her father called.

Morgan glanced back and saw him looking at her through the glass.

She pointed to the seaweed. "Do you know how this could have gotten all the way up here?"

"Seagull, probably," he said.

"Seagull?"

"Sure. He probably swooped down into the water to catch a fish and got a little seaweed as well. Then it fell as he was flying away."

"Oh . . ."

Could that be it? She was so on edge because of what she and Joel had discovered last night. It was possible that she'd imagined seeing the boy, and then started jumping to conclusions. Regardless, there was no point in arguing with her father, especially if he was about to take her to a place that could solve the problem.

"That makes sense, I guess," she told him.

"Sure. Now, if you want to do this today, let's go. Believe it or not, I do have other things on my agenda besides vanquishing evil spirits."

"Yeah, okay. Let's go."

She glanced at the seaweed on the railing one last time.

That's when she noticed the small sandy footprints.

As though a boy had recently perched there, looking through the glass doors into the house.

CHAPTER

THIRTEEN

Morgan tried to shake her dread by walking as fast as she could.

"Geez, I know I said I have things to do, but we don't have to rush *that* much." Her father wheezed as he tried to keep pace. He wasn't exactly the fittest guy in the world.

The air was cool and crisp, with the first hints that fall was coming. They walked past the old shipyard that had been converted to a park, and a bunch of restaurants that looked like they were trying a little too hard to be trendy New York bistros. Farther along the street she could see the Port Jefferson ferry, which transported people and cars back and forth to Connecticut.

But before they got to the ferry dock, Morgan's father led them down a side street, past a Realtor's office and a café. Finally they reached a cute little shop that had crystals, tie-dyed clothing, and other hippie stuff hanging in the window. In a flowing, curling font, the sign said:

Goddess by the Sea

It looked nice, but kind of cheesy, and definitely not like a place that sold anti-ghost gear.

"This is it?" Morgan didn't try to hide her disappointment.

"I'm not sure what you were expecting," said her father. "Van Helsing? Father Karras? Maybe John Constantine?"

"Who are those guys?"

He let out a pained sigh, which meant she was supposed to have somehow recognized some grown-up thing. "Never mind. This place will definitely have smudge sticks. You want one or not?"

"Yes."

"Well, then?" He opened the door and gestured for her to go inside.

The light in the shop was dim, and there was an odd sweet-spicy smell to the air. Gentle harp music played over the speakers. There were shelves full of candles, crystals, hemp bags, and rows of colorful scarves.

"Welcome, dear," said an old woman from behind the counter.

"Uh, hi," said Morgan.

The woman had long gray hair pulled back in a ponytail with a scarf. She wore a flowing purple-and-blue dress, and had earrings all the way up both sides of her ears. She had a gentle smile, but there was something sharp and searching about her gray eyes. Like she knew stuff. Maybe this was the right place after all.

"Hey there!" said Morgan's dad as he came in behind her. "We're looking for a smudge stick. You know, to keep away evil spirits and stuff."

The woman seemed to ignore him and instead continued to look at Morgan.

"There's no such thing as evil spirits," she said.

"Well, I told her that, but—" Morgan's father began.

The woman cut him off, her eyes still on Morgan. "Sad spirits? Yes. Angry spirits? You bet. But no spirit is truly *evil*."

"Oh," said Morgan, because she felt like she was supposed to respond somehow, and didn't know what else to say. She wondered if the woman would have said that if she knew it was a Nazi spirit.

"So you're having some spirit trouble?" the woman asked her.

"We, uh, live in the haunted house," Morgan said.

"Now, Morgan—" her father protested.

"Oh, yes, the haunted house," said the woman, cutting him off again. "I know which one you mean. Anyone who's lived here long enough knows that house."

Morgan's father looked surprised. "It's that well known in the neighborhood?"

The woman finally turned to him. "It is."

"Wow!" he said delightedly. "And you *really* think it's haunted?"

She gazed at him a moment, her expression amused. "It doesn't matter what I think." Then she turned back to Morgan. "So, a smudge stick to start?"

"I guess," said Morgan.

The woman nodded, then reached into a nearby glass case and pulled out a thick bundle of dried light-gray leaves tightly wrapped in twine.

"Light one end at the front door," instructed the woman. "Then move *slowly* clockwise around the entire house, into each room. Make certain to let the smoke drift into all the nooks and crannies, like closets and cupboards. It also might help to repeat a mantra that expresses your intentions while you do it."

"A mantra?" asked Morgan.

"Like a chant," said the woman. "As simply as you can, say out loud, over and over again, why you're doing this or what you hope will happen."

"Oh, okay . . ." The idea seemed goofy, but there was nothing goofy about the look in the old lady's eyes. "Thanks."

The woman nodded again.

Morgan paid for the smudge stick and they left.

"That was one cool old lady," her dad said brightly as they walked home.

"She really put you in your place," said Morgan.

"She sure did!" he agreed enthusiastically. "So cool!"

Morgan was pretty sure most dads would have gotten huffy and offended at being treated so rudely. But this was a classic response for her dad. It was like his head was so full of big ideas that he never took anything too personally.

"You're super weird, Dad."

He grinned at her. "Lucky you."

She couldn't help smiling back. After all, she wasn't exactly a normal Long Island girl like Hannah or Piper.

Once they got home, Morgan insisted that they do the smudging right away. She stood just inside the front door and lit one end of the bundle. It flamed a little at first, then settled down into a glowing orange ember that let off a pungent smell that was even stronger than when she'd lit the bowl of kitchen sage on fire.

"What mantra are you going to use?" asked her father.

"Oh, uh . . ." She hadn't actually been planning to do that part because it was a little embarrassing. But what if it was really important? "I just want the ghost to stay away from our house, so I guess . . . 'stay away'? Is that good enough?"

He shrugged. "I'm just a cartoonist. What do I know?"

She was about to begin, but then she looked over at her father. "Can you, uh . . . do something else right now?"

"Ah." He smiled knowingly. "Yeah, sure. I believe I owe you a Night Queen portrait anyway."

"Hey, yeah, that's right," she said. "*With* Kosuke."

"Right, right. Can't forget Dreamy McDreamboat. I'm off to work, then!"

Once her father was gone, she walked slowly from room to room, chanting "stay away" repeatedly. She felt a little silly. Especially since nothing really seemed to happen. Did it work? She had no idea. But she supposed it was better than doing nothing.

She felt even more embarrassed when she had to do her father's studio. But he kept his headphones on and continued to draw like she wasn't there, even though he had to be smelling the sage. She really appreciated that.

Morgan was just completing the full circuit of the house when her mother walked in through the front door.

"What is going on here?"

"I'm, uh, smudging," said Morgan awkwardly.

"Hey, hun!" Her father came out of his studio. "Did you know that our house is famous?"

"Oh?" Her mother's eyebrow rose.

"Yep, the whole town thinks of this as the local haunted house."

"Lovely," her mother said without enthusiasm. "And that's why we're burning sticks, is it?"

"Pretty much," he said cheerfully, acting like he didn't notice that she was annoyed. This was a normal tactic for him, and it usually worked. "Gotta get rid of them ghost Nazis, after all!"

Morgan's mother looked at them both for a moment, then sighed. "Honestly the two of you are so strange. Fine. If this is what it takes to put the whole thing behind us, smudge away."

Morgan finished up her smudging, then put out the stick in the sink.

"Feel better?" asked her mother.

"I do, actually," said Morgan, surprising herself. At least she didn't feel so helpless, and that had been the worst part.

And perhaps the smudging worked. That night there was no dripping, no crying, no seawater. She even checked the balcony the next morning and found that both the seaweed and the footprints were gone.

Had she really gotten rid of the ghost?

INTERLUDE

After a few weeks at the camp, Joseph noticed that some of the other boys began to behave differently. They talked about the "superior" Aryan race, just like the adults did. They only spoke in German, even when there were no adults around. In fact, they would tell on other kids who spoke English. They said it was for their own good, but Joseph watched their faces as kids were being punished, and he could tell they enjoyed it.

They also began to prey upon the weaker kids. Like Joseph.

He had tried to keep his nightly sobbing quiet, but apparently not quiet enough. The other boys started to call him "die heulsuse." The crybaby. But that was just the beginning. They told him that they'd *really* give him something to cry about. And soon after, they did.

They ambushed him by the outhouses one evening. He didn't know how many of them. More than he could count as he lay in the grass getting kicked repeatedly in the stomach. They kicked him until he threw up, then they called him disgusting and a disgrace to the Aryan race. They spat on him and ran away laughing.

He didn't know how long he lay there in the grass, but he was so miserable he couldn't bring himself to get up. It was nearly dark when one of the counselors from the girls' camp found him. Her name was Tillie Koch.

"Those boys are getting out of control," Tillie muttered as she helped him up. "Herr Dinkelacker needs to do something about them."

Herr Dinkelacker was the head of the entire Jungvolk, or youth camp. He was a tall, stern man with neatly combed blond hair. Joseph couldn't imagine ever telling him to do *anything*. He thought Tillie must be very brave to say such things out loud.

A few days later, Joseph learned she was willing to go much further than merely talking about it. He was hauling a wagon of bricks past the picnic tables and saw Tillie talking to another older girl who he didn't know.

"It's too much, Helen," Tillie told her. "Those boys

sneak over to the girls' tents at night and . . ." She shook her head, a pinched look crimping her face. "It's awful. It's *immoral* what they're doing."

Joseph knew some of the boys had started to sneak over to the girls' tents at night. He didn't know what they did there. He was mostly just grateful they weren't doing it to him.

"Didn't you talk to Herr Dinkelacker?" asked Helen.

"I did! And you know what he said? That what they're doing is perfectly natural! That I should be *pleased* we have such healthy German boys!"

"Horrible!" said Helen.

"Well," said Tillie, "if he won't put a stop to it, *I* will."

"How?" asked Helen.

"I'm going to keep watch tonight."

"All night?"

"*Every* night, if that's what it takes."

Helen chewed on her lip, looking worried. But she nodded.

That night, Joseph heard the boys sneak out of their tents as they had before. But they came back shortly after, muttering angrily to one another. That went on a for a few more nights, until the boys finally gave up. It looked like Tillie's plan had worked.

But then Tillie got sick from standing out in the chilly, damp field so many nights in a row. She developed a wet, rattling cough. It became hard for her to breathe, and a terrible fever left her half delirious.

Helen begged Herr Dinkelacker to fetch a doctor from town, but he refused.

"I will not pamper her," he declared. "She is not some soft American sissy. She has the mighty blood of *Germany* inside her!"

Five days later, Tillie Koch died.

FOURTEEN

Morgan was amazed at how much better she felt the next day. Maybe the smudging had gotten rid of the ghost for good, or maybe it was just temporary. Either way, she had done something, it worked, and that felt great. She wasn't some dumb girl in a horror story who needed rescuing. She was not helpless.

She felt so good that she decided to sit with the other girls at lunch again, and just hope they'd forgotten her ghost Nazi talk.

"Sup, new girl?" said Tressa as Morgan sat down.

"Hey," said Morgan.

She wondered if the other girls had even noticed that she hadn't sat there for the last couple of days. To be fair, it wasn't like she contributed much to the conversation. Partly that was because she found Hannah intimidating. But today Hannah hadn't shown up yet. It was just Tressa and Piper. Maybe that was what gave Morgan the courage to strike up a conversation.

"So . . . what do you guys do when you go into the city?"

"Oh, you know," said Piper. "See a Broadway show, go shopping on Fifth Avenue. Nothing special."

"Right . . ." Morgan had never seen a Broadway show. Her dad said it wasn't "real" theater, whatever that meant. And shopping for her was usually just the discount stores on Fulton Street.

"Piper, you do realize you're talking to a Brooklynite," pointed out Tressa. "Girl probably wouldn't be caught dead in a tourist trap like midtown Manhattan."

"I mean, I go to Manhattan sometimes," said Morgan. "Just . . ."

"Not above Fourteenth Street?" guessed Tressa.

Morgan laughed. "Pretty much. How'd you know that?"

"My sister goes to NYU, and she already acts like a city girl." Tressa sighed. "Every time she comes home to visit, she's got to make me jealous with all the cool stuff that goes on there." She flashed Morgan a smile. "Not like you, new girl. Maybe 'cause you grew up there you don't need to rub people's faces in it. I appreciate that, by the way."

"Oh, uh . . ." Morgan felt herself blushing a little.

"But still, Brooklyn . . ." Piper gave her trademark concerned frown. "Isn't it scary to live there?"

Morgan stared blankly. "Brooklyn? Scary?"

"All she knows about Brooklyn is from movies," said Tressa.

"Where I lived was mostly just families," Morgan assured Piper. "It's very chill."

It also didn't have any ghost Nazis, but Morgan wasn't going to mention that.

"Although they don't have wakeboarding," said Piper sympathetically. "You said you've never been."

"I've actually never even been on a boat," admitted Morgan.

Now it was Piper's turn to stare blankly. "I . . . don't understand. Like, no boat ever? In your *life*?"

"Does the Staten Island Ferry count?" Morgan asked.

Piper gravely shook her head.

Tressa laughed. "Yeah, for real. We have to fix that. After all, you're a Long Island girl now."

That was when Hannah sat down. "What do we have to fix?"

Morgan's stomach dropped. She'd been doing so well. It had actually started to feel like she belonged a little bit. Maybe she would have finally gotten an invitation to go boating with the girls. But she could already tell from the hard look in Hannah's eyes that wasn't going to happen now.

"Hannah," said Piper, "did you know that Morgan has never been on any kind of boat?"

"Huh, weird," said Hannah. "Anyway, who finished Mr. Thrush's homework? I did not get that last question at all."

And that was it. Once again, Morgan was pushed off to the side.

CHAPTER

FIFTEEN

Joel: Meet me when you get out of school

As Morgan was leaving school, she checked her phone and saw a message from Joel, along with an address. When she looked it up on the map, she saw that it was on the outskirts of the downtown area. Not exactly on the walk home, but not too far out of her way. At first she wondered why he wanted to meet there. Then she saw that the address was a place called the Port Jefferson Historical Society. Did he have a lead on what happened to Joseph Klaus?

Morgan wondered if that even mattered now. Maybe her smudging really had gotten rid of the ghost. If so, she could just forget this whole scary thing and move on with her life.

Although one haunt-free night didn't mean the ghost was gone for good. And it wasn't like Morgan could smudge the house on a weekly basis to keep it away. If nothing else, her mother would completely lose what little patience she currently had for the whole thing. So for now at least, it was probably best to keep investigating.

The reason that the Port Jefferson Historical Society was right on the edge of the downtown was because it was actually one of the old Victorian-style houses, complete with brightly painted shutters and a huge wraparound porch.

Joel was standing on the sidewalk in front of the house, his shaggy black hair in his face as he stared down at his phone.

"Hey," said Morgan.

"Oh, hey." He looked over at the house. "I called this place and there's supposedly a guy there who knows some stuff about the Nazi summer camp."

"Cool," said Morgan. "I smudged my house yesterday and so far it seems to be working."

"Smudged?" asked Joel.

"You burn a bundle of sage to get rid of spirits and stuff."

"Huh. And no haunting stuff last night?"

"Nope!"

"Well . . . that's good, right?" He looked like he was trying to be supportive, but for some reason he also looked concerned.

"Uh, yeah, obviously," she said. "Anyway, let's talk to this expert guy."

Now he seemed surprised, and a little relieved. "You still want to?"

"Joel, the ghost was *perching on my balcony* yesterday. I'm covering all my bases."

He looked even more relieved now. "Yeah, good idea."

The house was set a little back from the sidewalk, so they walked up a narrow, paved path to the front porch, then knocked on the door.

After a few moments, a tall man with a short white

beard, a fringe of white hair, and a bright red face opened the door.

"Ah, you must be the young scholars who called earlier!"

"Er, yeah . . ." said Joel. "We have a history project."

Morgan felt like ghost investigators sounded way better, but they probably needed to stick with the school project line so people didn't think they were "creepy weirdos."

"Wonderful! Come in, come in!"

The old man pushed open the door and gestured for them to enter.

"You're Mr. Johnson, then?" asked Joel as he and Morgan entered the house.

"*Professor* Johnson," the old man corrected him cheerfully. "I may be retired, but a true scholar never rests!"

"Right, sorry . . ." said Joel as he gazed around the interior.

It felt to Morgan like they'd stepped back in time. She wasn't sure to what time. Somewhere fancy, that was certain. Everything looked expensive and antique, from the faded pattern on the rug to the loudly ticking clock on the mantel above a massive fireplace.

"And you are?" asked Professor Johnson.

"Oh, I'm Joel, and this is Morgan."

"It's nice to meet you both. Why don't you have a seat while I go get some refreshments?" He gestured to a pink antique sofa with a dark wood frame. "Then we can get down to business."

"Uh, thanks."

Joel and Morgan sat down on the sofa, which was even less comfortable than it looked. The professor hurried out of the room, humming to himself, and they were left to sit in this strange time capsule.

"That is a really loud clock," Morgan remarked.

"It really is," agreed Joel.

They sat in awkward silence as the clock continued to thunder away. The place had an odd smell to it too. Like mothballs and medicine.

"I hope this wasn't a terrible idea," said Joel.

"Me too," said Morgan.

At last the professor returned with a tray of glasses and a pitcher of lemonade.

"Here we are, now!" He set the tray down on a small coffee table before them with a flourish. Morgan wondered if he'd made the lemonade specifically for them. She realized he was probably excited that kids were interested in history stuff. Well, if nothing else, they were cheering up a wacky old professor guy.

Professor Johnson poured them each a glass of lemonade, then sat back in a nearby chair that looked even less comfortable than the sofa. He took a swallow of his lemonade and let out a happy sigh.

"Ah! Refreshing!"

Morgan took a tentative sip from hers. She generally wasn't a huge fan of lemonade, but was surprised to find she really liked it.

"This is pretty good," she said. "Is it homemade?"

"Naturally," he said, looking pleased. Then he leaned toward them with an expectant look. "So, you want to learn about the history of Drowned Meadow, eh?"

"*Drowned* Meadow?" asked Morgan with a start.

The professor chuckled, looking even more pleased. "Oh, you didn't know? That was the original name for our little town, mainly because it used to flood on a regular basis. But then in the late eighteen hundreds they realized that it wasn't exactly a name that encouraged people to move here, so they changed it to Port Jefferson."

"That makes sense," said Joel. "Although it's not exactly Port Jefferson we're researching. We're trying to figure out what happened to Joseph Klaus."

"Ah." The old man gave them a knowing look. "Yes, quite an intriguing tale, isn't it?"

"You mean spooky," said Morgan.

Professor Johnson shrugged. "It amounts to the same thing."

Morgan wasn't so sure of that but decided not to argue. "So you know about Joseph Klaus?"

"Of course. I may be a historian, but I enjoy local legends as much as the next person."

"You mean about the haunted house?" asked Morgan. "That's my house."

"Is it?" asked the professor, no less delighted. "How exciting!"

"That's one way of putting it," said Morgan.

"There's something we're really confused about," said Joel. "What was up with the summer camp he was running away from?"

"Oh." The professor's smile faded. "I see."

"You know about that too?" asked Morgan.

"Camp Siegfried in Yaphank," said the professor darkly.

"Was it really a Nazi summer camp?" asked Joel.

The old man considered for a moment, swirling ice around in his lemonade glass.

"Don't think of it as a *summer camp* the way you understand them," he said finally. "These children had no time for fun and games. They were only allowed to speak German. If they didn't know it, they had to learn it fast. And they were taught Nazi ideology—that Germans were superior to everyone else in the world, that the Jews were evil and must be eradicated. They were told that everyone should obey Der Führer, or the leader, without question. And those weren't even the worst things that happened to the poor children who attended the camp."

He paused for a moment and scratched his white beard thoughtfully. It seemed like he was still trying to decide how much to tell them.

"The children were abused in a number of ways," he

said at last. "They were forced to go on extended hikes all night long carrying twenty-pound packs, often with little nourishment. They were also forced to lay bricks when the camp wanted a new building, because it was believed that all the construction companies were controlled by Jews. And if any of the kids complained or cried, they were beaten for showing weakness."

"How awful . . ." said Morgan. Until that moment, she had only been thinking of Joseph Klaus as the scary Nazi ghost. But what the professor was saying reminded her of what Joel had said a few nights before. That Joseph had been so desperate to escape Camp Siegfried that he'd died trying to get home. Maybe he hadn't been some horrible Nazi boy. Maybe he'd actually been one of their victims.

"And I'm afraid Siegfried was more than a mere camp for children," continued the professor. "It was an entire Nazi *community* right in the heart of Long Island. Some people lived there, and many others came to visit regularly."

"A community?" Joel looked completely spooked. "Like . . . how *many* Nazis are we talking about?"

Johnson poured himself some more lemonade as he spoke. "At one point Camp Siegfried was so popular that there was a train on the Long Island Rail Road that ran every weekend called the Siegfried Special. It brought people from all over New York City. When they arrived, they were welcomed by uniformed men with Nazi flags, and sometimes even a marching band. Then they would all march through town back to the camp, goose-stepping the whole way."

Morgan had a vivid imagination, but even she struggled to picture a group of uniformed Nazis marching down Port Jefferson's Main Street. "What were the grown-ups doing at the camp?"

Johnson leaned back and took a sip of his lemonade before speaking. "I imagine some people were just there to dance and drink. There was a traditional German beer hall on the premises, and since many of the older members emigrated from Germany after the First World War, they were probably looking for a comforting reminder of their homeland, and people who spoke in their native tongue. However, there were others, mostly young men, who trained rigorously in firearms and explosives."

"Like an army?" asked Morgan. "But why?"

The professor leaned toward them, his expression grave. "They were preparing both themselves and the children who went to the camp for what they referred to as 'Der Tag.'"

"Der Tag?" asked Joel.

"It means 'The Day.'"

"The day of what?" pressed Morgan.

"The day they planned to overthrow democracy," said the professor. "And turn America into a fascist dictatorship under the control of Adolf Hitler."

INTERLUDE

Joseph Klaus did not understand what was happening. He stood with the other boys at the funeral of Tillie Koch, which was held at Camp Siegfried, and listened to Herr Dinkelacker talk about her as though her death had been somehow important to the Nazi cause. He called her a hero and martyr, and said she had brought glory to the German people. But Joseph couldn't see how that was true.

He looked at Tillie's dad, who stood beside her casket, face creased with sorrow, his hands clutching his wool cap. Joseph wondered if *he* saw any glory in his daughter's death. It didn't seem like it. And when Joseph looked over at the group of girls who went to the camp, they were all huddled together, fighting back the tears they were not allowed to shed. Yet the boys who stood with him all gazed at Dinkelacker with clear, untroubled expressions. Obviously *they* believed him.

Once Dinkelacker had dismissed everyone, Joseph

nervously approached Tillie's friend Helen. The older girl stared at the casket with hard eyes.

"Is it true?" Joseph whispered in English. "Was Tillie a martyr for the Nazi cause?"

Helen's mouth twisted, as though she'd just tasted something unpleasant. "Don't you believe it, kid."

Then she turned and walked away.

Soon after, the boys were summoned to stand at attention in the field before Herr Dinkelacker, who stood erect in his pristine Nazi uniform and gave them an icy stare.

"There have been *complaints* about your behavior," he said in German.

There were several seconds of silence, during which some of the boys nervously shifted their weight. Joseph thought they *should* be nervous. After all, it was partly their fault that Tillie had died. Did this mean they would finally get punished? He didn't like that it took something so sad, but maybe the boys would stop picking on people.

Eventually Dinkelacker continued. "It is natural for you to express yourselves in this way, but you must not be so *obvious*. Some people have become too soft and Americanized, and they have forgotten what is right and proper behavior for healthy Aryan boys."

Joseph stared at the camp director, somewhere between shock and horror.

"From now on, I expect you to be *discreet*. You will take your activities into the woods where others cannot see," said Dinkelacker. "Is that understood?"

"Yes, sir!" shouted the other boys with obvious relief. Perhaps even eagerness.

But Joseph only felt dread. The bullies had been given permission to carry on with whatever they wanted to do. What would that mean for him, "die heulsuse"?

CHAPTER SIXTEEN

For the second night in a row, Morgan didn't experience any hauntings. Was the ghost really gone? Did it only take a little burning sage and some chanting?

"It seems too easy," said Joel when they met up the following day after school at the ice-cream shop.

"Right?" asked Morgan. "But the last time someone lived in the house, there wasn't much internet. They couldn't just do a search online for ghost stuff like I did. Maybe they didn't know about the sage."

"It sounds like that old lady you talked to at the shop knew," pointed out Joel.

Morgan shrugged. "Maybe nobody asked her. She *is* kind of intimidating."

"Hmm . . ." Joel stirred his milkshake with a straw, then took a sip.

"I haven't even been having nightmares anymore," said Morgan.

"You were having nightmares?" asked Joel. "You never mentioned that."

"Yeah." Morgan thought back to that moment she'd pulled a strand of seaweed out of her mouth and shuddered. "They're not really something I want to think about, much less talk about."

"That bad, huh?" he asked.

She nodded.

He tapped the top of his straw thoughtfully. "So do you think the ghost was trying to let you know how he felt?"

"I hadn't thought of it that way, but maybe."

"Don't forget," said Joel, "that old lady told you there's no such thing as evil spirits."

"Just sad ones and angry ones," said Morgan. "When the professor was telling us about all the awful stuff that happened at the camp, I realized that Joseph might have run away because it was so terrible."

"Yeah," said Joel. "He could have been like Vladja in *My Secret Dream of a Boring Life*."

Morgan thought about the comparison between Joseph and Vladja for a moment. Vladja was a young vampire who joined the Night Queen's court in volume five. He was from a kingdom of undead called Nezhit. He fled his homeland because the rulers had been treating their subjects badly, and when he objected to their cruelty, they tried to lock him in a coffin forever. He barely managed to escape, and found protection with the Night Queen.

"I guess the difference," she said finally, "is that Joseph died before he reached safety."

"Does that make him sad or angry?" wondered Joel.

"Maybe both."

They were quiet for a moment. Morgan took a slow sip of her egg cream, while Joel continued to fiddle with the straw on his milkshake.

Then suddenly he said, "We should go to Yaphank."

"Huh?" Morgan gave him a baffled look. "Why?"

"Don't you want to see where it all happened?" he asked anxiously.

"But Camp Siegfried isn't even there anymore, right?" asked Morgan.

"No," admitted Joel. "Apparently it's just a regular community called German Gardens now. And they changed the street names too, of course. So there's no more Adolf Hitler Street."

"Then what would be the point?" asked Morgan.

Joel frowned. "I don't know . . . I just want to make sure, I guess."

"Make sure of what?" asked Morgan.

"I don't know!" For some reason Joel seemed upset. He kept twirling his straw in the milkshake, and his lips were pressed into a thin line.

"Okay, okay. Jeez, relax," said Morgan.

He sighed. "Sorry. I guess because I'm Jewish, this whole thing really freaks me out. And I thought maybe if I faced this fear . . . you know? Like . . ." He shook his head. "It's a dumb idea. Never mind."

"I didn't realize you were Jewish," said Morgan.

"Come on." He raised an eyebrow. "The name Joel Applebaum wasn't enough for you?"

She shrugged. "I just never thought about it. Anyway, I guess it makes sense that Nazi stuff would freak you out even more than me. Did you have any family in the Holocaust?"

"Yeah." His expression was oddly neutral, so Morgan couldn't really tell how he felt about it.

"Sorry," she said.

He gave her a wan smile. "Thanks."

She wanted to ask more. She'd never talked to anybody who'd had family in something like the Holocaust before. But it felt like he really didn't want to talk about it. It was clearly something that bothered him a lot. She felt a little guilty for bringing it up, so she changed back to the original subject.

"If you really want to go to Yaphank . . ."

He shook his head. "No, it was a dumb idea. Forget about it."

"Okay . . ."

Was he just saying that because he was embarrassed and didn't want to drag her along? She didn't know.

There felt like a strange separation between them. Like he was holding back in a way he hadn't before. She wondered, was it because he was Jewish and he thought there were things that she'd just never understand?

Were there things that she would never understand?

CHAPTER · SEVENTEEN

This new distance between Morgan and Joel made her feel lonely in a way she hadn't since before that first night they'd talked at the ice-cream shop. He was basically her only real friend. Although that friendship had been built around the ghost problem. Now that she seemed to have solved it, would they still hang out? She wasn't sure. It wasn't like she normally hung out with boys. And he didn't even go to her school.

She had another night free of haunting, so that was good at least. The ghost really did seem to have taken the hint and left. Although something about that bothered her . . . Maybe she was a little disappointed that there hadn't been some big anime-style show-down with the supernatural. Well, she was no anime hero, so that was probably for the best. And now she could focus on trying to make friends with the girls at her school.

The opportunity came even sooner than she'd expected. It was a Saturday afternoon, and her mother decided to drag her to the grocery store to "air out the offspring" as she liked to put it. Morgan's mother was one of those active types who didn't really consider reading all day to be *doing* something. She also claimed that Morgan was a "big help" who made the trip to the store "so much faster," but Morgan was unconvinced. She and her mother would split the shopping list in half—"divide and conquer," her mother called it. It made sense in theory. But in reality, any time Morgan saved was probably spent trying to locate her mother in the ridiculously large grocery stores that were apparently standard on Long Island.

It was while she was lugging her basket of groceries around the store, looking for her mother, that she ran into Piper. She was standing in the back of the store by the restrooms.

"Hey, Piper." Morgan thought that she was probably the least intimidating of the three girls, since she wasn't as aggressive as Hannah or as cool as Tressa.

Piper smiled in that anxious way of hers. "Oh, hey, Morgan."

This was the first time one of the three girls had called her by name, and she thought that might be a good sign.

"Are you here shopping with your mom too?" Morgan asked.

"Huh? Uh, no, I'm with—"

"Hey, new girl."

The voice came from behind Morgan, but there was no mistaking that harsh, competitive tone.

"Hey, Hannah."

Morgan had been hoping to chat with Piper alone, but she tried not to show her disappointment as she turned to face the other girl.

Hannah grinned at her in a way that looked almost malicious. Then she said, "How's your creepy weirdo *boyfriend?*"

Morgan stared at her, alarm rising in her chest.

"Hannah . . ." mumbled Piper. "You promised you wouldn't . . ."

"I'm just *curious*," said Hannah, her expression oddly triumphant. "It's been so long since I've talked to Joel Applebaum that I thought I'd ask his *girlfriend* how he's doing."

"Joel is *not* my boyfriend!" objected Morgan, trying not to show the panic she was feeling.

"No?" Hannah asked, not looking convinced. "That's funny, since Piper saw the two of you practically *making out* on your ice-cream date yesterday."

"We weren't on a date, and we definitely were *not* almost making out," insisted Morgan.

Hannah gave a big dramatic shrug. "I'm just taking Piper's word for it. Are you saying she's lying?"

"M-Maybe I misinterpreted . . ." muttered Piper, her eyes downcast and her pale face turning red.

Morgan wheeled on her, the panic turning to anger. "I don't know what you think you saw, but we're definitely not dating."

"But you *are* hanging out with the creepy weirdo,

then?" Hannah's eyes gleamed, like a predator going in for the kill. "You guys are like BFFs or something?"

"No, we were just . . ."

She couldn't use the history project excuse because Piper and Hannah were *in* her history class. So she'd either have to tell them about the whole ghost Nazi thing, or else lie. And right there in the middle of a grocery store, with Hannah smirking at her, the ghost Nazi thing seemed pretty ridiculous. It was likely to earn her the nickname Mrs. Creepy Weirdo.

"Look . . ." she said, feeling her way through an idea. "My mom kind of made me do it. He's the only other kid our age on my block and she said I had to be nice to him. So when he asked me if I wanted to go get ice cream, I kind of had to say yes."

"Hmm . . ." Hannah's eyes narrowed, like she wasn't sure whether to believe this. And with good reason. If she knew Morgan's mother, she'd know this was not something that would ever happen.

Piper bought it immediately. "Your mom made you hang out with him? That's horrible!"

"Well, it's not like I had anything better to do." That part, at least, was true.

Hannah still looked suspicious. "So you're telling me that—"

"There you are, Morgan."

All three of them turned to see Morgan's mother pushing a grocery cart toward them. Morgan realized this could be a potential disaster if Hannah decided to question her mother about this supposedly forced ice-cream hangout. She needed to get out of there before that happened.

"Hey, Mom, here's the rest of the stuff." She quickly put her basket of groceries in with the rest. "Let's go."

Her mom looked over at Piper and Hannah. "You want to introduce me to your friends?"

"Oh, uh . . ." Morgan looked over at Piper, who was somehow able to look both embarrassed and quietly judgmental, and Hannah, who looked like she was still trying to find a hole in Morgan's excuse. The Mrs. Creepy Weirdo label would not be so easy to escape.

Basically, just as she'd feared it might, guilt-by-association with Joel had killed her social life.

Morgan put on an indifferent expression and shrugged. "This is Piper and Hannah. We're just class-mates. Can we go?"

Thankfully her mother seemed to pick up on the tension and didn't push it any further.

"Well, girls," her mother said with that forced brightness she reserved for uncomfortable situations. "Have a great day!"

"You too, Mrs. Calvino," Piper said. "See you at school, Morgan."

"Sure," said Morgan. "See you around."

Once they were out of earshot, her mother mur-mured, "What was *that* about?"

"That," said Morgan, "was another doomed attempt at making friends in Long Island."

"Ah," said her mother.

CHAPTER

EIGHTEEN

When Morgan and her mother got home, she couldn't quite settle down. The scene in the grocery store played over and over in her head, each time just a little more embarrassing. The thing was, she'd always known something like this could happen. But over time, she'd gotten so comfortable with Joel that she kind of forgot. He'd texted her to meet at the ice-cream shop after school, and she'd been bored, so she said yes without even thinking about it. Dumb.

Her mom got a work call soon after they arrived home, and her dad was in his studio, so Morgan was on her own with her anxious misery. She tried to read but couldn't focus. Even watching TV couldn't hold her attention. Eventually she ended up sitting on the balcony with a can of coconut seltzer, staring moodily out over the water.

Joel: You want to meet at the ice cream shop?

Morgan looked down at the text message. It was almost exactly the same as the one from yesterday. But this time she wasn't going to automatically say okay. What reason did they even have to hang out anymore? The ghost was gone, case closed.

Morgan: not feeling ice cream tonight

She hadn't wanted to be completely rude, so she'd made it sound like it was just tonight. But really, when would they ever hang out again? Maybe he'd just stop asking . . .

Joel: ok

Morgan wondered if that was it. But a few moments after she put her phone down, it pinged again.

Joel: The new Infamous Motley movie is in theaters this weekend. You want to see it tomorrow?

That was actually a tempting invitation. She wasn't a hardcore *Infamous Motley* fan, but she'd watched the first season of the anime and it was pretty fun. And there was always something special about seeing an anime movie in a theater with a bunch of other anime and manga fans. It could be a fun, boisterous experience, with everyone cheering the protagonist on. At least, that's how it had been in Brooklyn anyway. She had no idea how it was out on Long Island.

But as much as she wanted to go, if Morgan was spotted in the movie theater lobby with Joel, that would squash any remaining hope of making friends at Port Jeff Middle.

What should she tell him, though? He already knew she liked the show, so she couldn't pretend she didn't. She could just say she was busy, but then he might ask with what, and then she'd have to keep digging in deeper on the lie. She didn't want to lie to Joel.

She could just tell him straight up that she didn't want to hang out with him, but she couldn't think of any way to say that without sounding horrible.

In the end, she simply didn't respond.

Later that night she checked the Night Queen chat server. Everyone was raving about the *Infamous Motley* movie. Including Madison.

MadMadison: for real prob the best anime film I've ever seen in my life

Morgan stared at the post, feeling her stomach churn. Madison had still not responded to *any* of her texts. She didn't know why, but clearly her ex–best friend was ghosting her. It was an awful feeling. She knew it was called "ghosting" because the person seemed to disappear. But it also made *her* feel like a ghost. Like she was invisible and inaudible. Like she didn't matter.

Then it dawned on Morgan that *she* had ghosted Joel.

She slowly closed the lid on her laptop and stared at her phone, which lay on her bed. It was too late to reply now, wasn't it? And anyway, what would she say? There was still that same problem. If he asked why she didn't want to go, she'd either have to make something up or tell him the truth. Even though she'd lied her pants off to Hannah and Piper, she didn't want to do that to Joel for some reason. But she also didn't want to have to tell him that she couldn't hang out with him because he was killing her social life.

Maybe he didn't really care. She could be making a bigger deal out of it than it really was.

And maybe Madison had told herself the same thing, so she didn't feel bad about ignoring Morgan.

INTERLUDE

Joseph Klaus's life became much harder after the death of Tillie Koch. The other boys decided that being "discreet" meant they couldn't all sneak over to the girls' tents together. So they agreed to take turns, with only a few going each night. Those who remained behind were still anxious and eager to express the "proper behavior for healthy Aryan boys." And naturally some of them turned to the victim closest at hand: die heulsuse.

He tried to stand up to them the first time. He told them as firmly as he could to leave him alone. They only laughed and punched him in the stomach. Then they dragged him out of the tent and into a nearby wooded area, where they kicked him until he threw up, all the while telling him it was for his own good. If he wanted to survive Der Tag, he would have to toughen up and start acting like a proper Aryan. When they were finished, they would drag him half unconscious back to the tent and toss him onto his bed, where others would stare and sometimes make fun of him. But by then, the pain and fear had left him numb to any further shame.

It was different boys every night, but nearly the same thing happened. As though it was a play they were all rehearsing. Except there was nothing pretend about the bruises he accrued. And there was no one he could ask for help. Tillie was gone. Helen had been transferred to Camp Nordland in New Jersey, where older teens received more intense training and education. There was even talk of her being sent to train with the *real* Hitler Youth in Germany. So Joseph was all alone.

He had to escape Camp Siegfried. Otherwise he would end up dead, just like Tillie.

For weeks he didn't know how he would do it. Each day he endured the forced marches, the bricklaying, and the hours of lectures about the great Führer's plan for world domination. Each night he endured the beatings and mockery.

Then at last he saw it. A delivery truck parked near the entrance. The back was covered with a tarp. He just had to find the right moment to slip away, then hide on the truck without being noticed. When it left, it would take him with it. Where? It didn't even matter to him anymore. Anywhere was better than here.

The opportunity came at midday. The boys were led on a march with their weighted backpacks. As usual, it was hot and uncomfortable. Briars slashed at their bare arms and legs as they marched through woods and across fields, their empty stomachs growling. They weren't supposed to show their discomfort, of course, but sometimes Joseph couldn't help it. And when he showed even a little bit of weakness, it infuriated some of the other boys. Finally, as they hiked along a hilltop under the blazing sun, one of them looked over at the misery written plainly on Joseph's face and sneered. Then the boy kicked Joseph's legs out from under him. He tumbled down the hill, his twenty-pound pack pulling him on until he landed with a crunch in a thistle patch.

Joseph could hear their laughter. He heard the adult call down to him, telling him to stop napping. But he didn't move. The adult threatened to leave him behind. He struggled half-heartedly, but still didn't rise. Finally the adult gave up in disgust and ordered the group to continue on without him.

Once they were out of sight, Joseph abandoned his weighted pack and ran as fast as he could back the way they'd come. They were more than halfway through the hike, so he had farther to go. But without the pack he practically flew across the fields, making it back to the camp well before the others.

He looked over to the entrance and saw with relief that the truck was still there. He considered going back to the tent for his few belongings, but decided it wasn't worth the risk. Instead he picked up a nearby crate and walked as casually as he could, hoping it looked like he was supposed to be loading cargo onto the truck. Not that the few adults sitting at a nearby table drinking beer paid him any mind.

Once he reached the truck, he lifted the tarp, slid in the crate, and then, after one last glance back to the adults at the table, clambered in and pulled the tarp down after him.

CHAPTER

NINETEEN

The story arc for volume seven of *My Secret Dream of a Boring Life* was Morgan's least favorite in the entire series. One of the things she loved most about the series overall was how all the strange and disparate characters from different races and worldviews somehow got along. But in volume seven, their odd, happy extended family fell apart.

It started off as an argument between Zophia and Kosuke, when he realized that in order to conquer the kingdom, she'd had to kill a lot of humans—and worse, that she didn't feel bad about it at all. Zophia believed she'd done what she had to in order to protect the non-human races, and she wasn't going to apologize for it. Their argument spread across the court, everyone picking sides. Things got so bad that Zophia and Kosuke stopped talking to each other altogether.

After that, Zophia Zye felt lonelier than ever, because now she knew what it was like to have real friends. In her sadness, she went back to being the haughty, cold Night Queen from volume one, but it didn't feel cool anymore. She'd been through so much and come so far. It just felt like she was taking the easy way out.

Morgan sighed and let the open book fall over her face. She could skip this volume and jump right to number eight. It wasn't like she didn't remember what happened. But that felt like *she* was taking the easy way out too. And she knew that the payoff in eight would feel so much better if she made it through seven.

She was sprawled out on the couch in the living room, so when the doorbell rang, she was the closest person to the front door. By family decree, that meant she had to answer it. She groaned and pushed herself up off the couch, then trudged across the living room to the door.

When she opened it, she was greeted by a blast of heat. Even though it was early September, they were having one of those last-ditch temperature jumps, like summer was having one final hurrah before autumn got serious.

She didn't know who she expected to be at the door. But it definitely wasn't Tressa.

"Oh," said Morgan, straightening up a little. "Hey."

Tressa grinned. "Hey, new girl. Hot enough for you?"

"You want to come in?" asked Morgan.

"You want to come out?" countered Tressa.

"Huh?"

Tressa pointed across the street to where a large boat sat tied to the dock.

"Is that yours?" asked Morgan.

"Yup. You said you've never been wakeboarding, right? Well, today is a perfect day for it and my mom is taking us out. So are you in?"

"For real?" asked Morgan.

Tressa rolled her eyes. "No, we came all this way just to troll you. So can you come or what?"

"Uh . . . let me check."

"And change into a swimsuit," Tressa called as Morgan hurried back into the house.

Her father was in the kitchen, attempting to learn how to bake something. Morgan did not have high hopes for the outcome, since he had never baked anything in his life.

"Dad, can I go wakeboarding with some girls from school?"

"Say what now?" He stared at her, the mixing bowl cradled in one arm, his other hand frozen in mid-stir. She supposed she couldn't blame him, since she had never asked for anything like this before. "Uh . . . will there be an adult there?"

"Tressa's mom."

"I guess . . . cool then?" He still seemed a little confused.

"Thanks, Dad!"

"S-Sure . . ."

She hurried up to her room and got changed into a

swimsuit, then pulled her shorts on and a T-shirt over that. As she made her way back down, she called out to her father.

"See you later!"

"Have fun! Be home for dinner! It's going to be amazing!"

She glanced doubtfully at the doughy substance he was shoveling into a pan. "Er . . . can't wait!"

Morgan returned to Tressa, and the two crossed the street toward the dock.

"Hey," said Tressa. "Sorry about my clueless friends."

"Oh . . . I guess you heard about all that with Joel?"

"Yeah. They were like, can you believe she was hanging out with him, and I was like, hello, she literally just told you it was because she didn't have anything better to do. And that is just *sad*!" Tressa shook her head. "I didn't even think about it before, but here we were talking at lunch every day about boating and wakeboarding and all of that, and you're just sitting there patiently waiting to be invited."

Morgan gave an embarrassed laugh. "Uh, yeah, it did cross my mind."

"And we totally missed it!" said Tressa. "But don't worry. I got you. From now on, we'll make sure you're way too busy for your mom to be sending you on dates with Joel Applebaum."

"It really wasn't a date," said Morgan.

"I bet *Joel* thought it was," said Tressa.

"R-really?"

"Of course."

Morgan hadn't thought about that before, but maybe it was true. He'd invited her to see a movie with him, which for a middle schooler was about as close to a proper date as you could get.

"Oh, wow . . ." she said out loud.

Tressa gave her a knowing look. "I thought you Brooklyn types were supposed to be *worldly*."

"Only about some things, I guess," said Morgan.

Tressa's boat was a motorboat rather than a sailboat. It looked like a sleek white dart with a blue awning that covered the cockpit.

"Ahoy there!" called a middle-aged Black woman who sat at the steering wheel. "Welcome aboard, Morgan!"

"Uh, thanks, Ms. Witherspoon," said Morgan as she

awkwardly straddled the open space between the dock and the shifting boat.

"I hear this is your first time on a boat," said Tressa's mom.

"Yep."

"Well, have a seat while we get underway. Tressa, can you cast us off?"

"Sure thing." Tressa remained on the dock and began to untie the ropes that held the boat in place.

Morgan sat down on a white cushioned seat across from Ms. Witherspoon. Once Tressa had untied the ropes, she stepped on. Her mom pulled some levers, spun the silver wheel, then guided the boat away from the dock and out into the harbor.

There was a cabin below the front, and once they were underway, Piper and Hannah emerged from inside.

"Uh, hey, Morgan," said Piper. Morgan couldn't tell if she felt bad about the day before—Piper sort of always looked anxious.

"Okay, landlubber!" Hannah said boisterously, clearly not feeling bad at all. "If you're going to be a proper

Long Island girl, I guess I'll have to teach you how it's done."

Morgan suspected that was probably as good an apology as she was going to get. So she just smiled.

"Cool."

CHAPTER TWENTY

Ms. Witherspoon guided the boat slowly so as not to cause too much wake for all the other vessels moored around them. After gliding for several more minutes through the crowded harbor, they finally emerged into Long Island Sound and began to pick up speed.

The boat skimmed along the surface, kicking up a light spray on either side. The immense stretch of water before them glittered in the midday sun. When Morgan had looked at the sound on a map, it seemed dinky compared to the Atlantic Ocean. But now it filled her entire vision. She could see nothing else beyond it, and for the first time she thought she might understand the true scale of the ocean. It was beautiful, but also a little frightening in its vastness.

Hannah and Tressa were clearly very comfortable with it all. Once the boat was speeding through the sound, they stripped down to their swimsuits. Then they clambered up to the front of the boat, where they could stretch out beneath the sun. There were small metal railings on either side, so it wasn't completely unsafe, and Ms. Witherspoon didn't seem concerned. But Morgan decided to stay in the cockpit with Piper under the blue canopy.

Piper gave one of her anxious smiles and tugged at the sleeve of her T-shirt. "It doesn't matter how much sunscreen I put on. I always burn."

"Oh, I totally forgot sunscreen," said Morgan.

Ms. Witherspoon pointed to a large canvas bag nestled against the seat beside her. "In the bag."

"Ms. Witherspoon thinks of everything," said Piper.

"That's what a mom does," said Ms. Witherspoon.

Piper smiled again but didn't respond. There was something about her expression that made Morgan wonder if her own mother wasn't like that.

"There's also snacks if you get hungry," continued Ms. Witherspoon. "And make sure you hydrate. There's a cooler with waters in the cabin."

"Thanks, Ms. Witherspoon," said Morgan.

"If this is your first time on a boat, I want it to be a good experience," she said.

They cruised through the sound for a little while. The sun shone down brightly from the clear blue sky, but the canopy shielded Morgan from direct light, and the ocean breeze blew strongly through her hair. She was surprisingly comfortable.

"Does your family have a boat?" Morgan asked Piper.

"Yeah," she said. "But it's, like, a serious racing boat."

"I don't even know the difference," confessed Morgan.

"Oh . . ." Piper looked surprised, like she'd assumed everyone knew the difference between a "regular" boat and a "serious racing" boat. Then she smiled, but this time it was more relaxed and confident than usual. "Well, this is a powerboat, and my dad's is a sailboat, which wouldn't be great for wakeboarding. A large sailboat also needs a crew of people. When we take it out, it's all hands. You can't just hang out like this. You have to help out, and you have to know what you're doing, or it can be dangerous."

"Dangerous?" asked Morgan.

Piper's expression became serious, and even more self-assured. "Sailing is fun, but you always have to be safe. My dad says that even the saltiest sailor shouldn't take the sea for granted. If you get sloppy or stop paying attention, you could fall overboard, and that might be it for you. The sea is a cruel mistress, he always says. And if you're not careful, she'll take you."

"R-Really . . . ?" Morgan glanced out at the rippling waters that surrounded them. There was nothing else in sight. No lifeguards or floats, and no land. How deep *was* it out here?

"But don't worry!" Piper patted her arm reassuringly, as if only now realizing that what she said might be freaking Morgan out. "We'll be safe. I promise!"

"You got that right," said Ms. Witherspoon as she slowed the boat down. "And everybody's wearing life jackets, no complaints." She gave her daughter and Hannah a hard look, then raised her voice to make sure they could hear her. "That goes *double* for the danger twins."

Tressa waved her hand in acknowledgment and Hannah heaved a dramatic sigh. Morgan wondered if they were wearing life jackets for her sake, or if this was a regular argument with Tressa's mom.

"Okay, this looks like a good spot," Ms. Witherspoon decided, although to Morgan it didn't look any different from the previous ten minutes of open water. "Jackets on, everyone."

The bright yellow life vests were stored under the bench at the back of the cockpit. When Morgan put hers on and clipped the front shut, it felt uncomfortable and a little cumbersome. She could understand why Tressa and Hannah weren't thrilled about wearing them. But Morgan also found its bulk reassuring.

"I'd better go first, to show the new girl how it's done," asserted Hannah.

"You mean so you can show off," said Tressa.

Hannah didn't seem shamed by that at all. "Same thing."

The wakeboard looked like a surfboard, except shorter—only about four feet long. There were what looked like rubber boots fastened to the board to keep the rider's feet in place. Hannah sat down on a narrow platform on the back of the boat, or the "stern," which Ms. Witherspoon said was the proper name for the rear of the boat.

Tressa handed Hannah the wakeboard and she fastened her feet to it. Then Piper handed her a long rope with a handle attached to the end.

Once she was all set, Hannah slid into the water. She bobbed up and down on the surface, kept up by her life jacket and the wakeboard, and gradually drifted away from the boat.

"Hannah, you ready?" called Ms. Witherspoon.

Hannah positioned herself so the board was between her and the boat, then gripped the rope handle with both hands.

"Ready!" she called, and gave a thumbs-up.

Ms. Witherspoon pushed on a lever and the boat began to speed up. Morgan watched as Hannah, her knees bent, slowly rose on the board. At first the board was still perpendicular to the boat, but once she was fully standing, she twisted so that it was pointing forward. She gave a thumbs-up again. Ms. Witherspoon nodded and increased the boat's speed.

"Oh, right," Tressa said. "Morgan, give a thumbs-up whenever you want my mom to speed up, or a thumbs-down if you want her to slow down. And if you want her to stop, go like this." She made a back-and-forth cutting motion in front of her neck.

"Got it," said Morgan.

"And do me a favor," said Ms. Witherspoon. "If you fall, tap your head so I know you're okay."

"Will do," Morgan promised, feeling that familiar tickle of anxiety at having to perform athletically in front of other people. She was famously clumsy, and always seemed to have scrapes on her arms and legs with no idea where she got them. Once, when she was younger, she gave herself a black eye by running headfirst into a shopping cart. Another time, she somehow chipped a tooth while climbing up the ladder at the pool. So she was pretty sure she wouldn't be great at wakeboarding. But this was clearly a thing Long Island girls did, so here she was, hoping she at least didn't make a complete fool of herself.

Hannah made wakeboarding look so easy. She glided along the surface of the water, shifting back and forth from one side to the other. After a little while, she gave another thumbs-up, and Ms. Witherspoon increased the boat's speed even more.

Now that the boat was going faster, it was beginning to kick up more wake behind it. But rather than letting the foamy white ripples throw her off, Hannah used them as ramps and began jumping. Just little jumps at first, then higher ones. She started twisting the board, changing which foot was forward while she was in midair.

"Here we go." Tressa rolled her eyes, but she was also clearly enjoying the show.

"She really is so good," said Piper.

"Can you do that stuff?" Morgan asked as they

watched Hannah leap and twist gracefully across the frothy surface.

"No way," said Piper. "If I can go the whole time without falling, I'm happy."

"It's a lot harder than she makes it look," said Tressa.

"Hannah is a natural athlete," agreed her mom. "Although you're not too shabby yourself."

Tressa shrugged.

Eventually Hannah did the cutting motion and Tressa's mom gradually brought the boat to a halt. Hannah used the rope to pull herself back to the boat, then Tressa and Piper helped her up onto the platform.

"And *that's* how it's done, new girl," declared Hannah as she unstrapped her feet from the board.

Morgan really wished Hannah would stop calling her that, but she smiled. "You were amazing."

Hannah seemed pleased by that. "Okay, Tress, let's see what you got."

Tressa was also very good, although not as flashy with her tricks as Hannah. She seemed more interested in speed. She got her mom to go even faster than she'd gone with Hannah. Piper wasn't as flashy either, or even that interested in going fast. She seemed content to simply glide along at a relaxed pace, which Morgan thought sounded like an excellent plan when her turn came.

"Okay, new girl," Hannah said as Morgan sat down on the platform and strapped her feet to the board. "Just remember, don't lock your knees, and keep your center of gravity over the board. Do those two things and you'll be fine."

Morgan smiled to cover her mounting tension. She wondered what it would feel like to have a body that just obeyed her like that. "Sure."

She carefully slid into the water, and despite the heat of the day, it was so cold it made her catch her breath.

Piper handed her the rope with the handle. "Good luck!"

"You want to go about as far back as the rope will let you," advised Tressa.

The surface rippled with the wind, and Morgan was

already drifting away. To hurry it along, she awkwardly used the half-submerged board to push farther away until finally she was quite far from the boat.

"Let me know when you're ready, Morgan," Ms. Witherspoon said.

Morgan couldn't see any point in delaying. She would only get more nervous. So she bent her knees and drew the board up, like she'd seen the other girls do. Then she gave the thumbs-up. The boat's engine revved, the rope went taut, and Morgan was pulled forward.

Over her board. Face-first into the water.

She was afraid the boat would drag her along face-down, but fortunately Ms. Witherspoon saw immediately what had happened and cut the motor.

As Morgan struggled to right herself, Tressa's mom called, "You okay, Morgan?"

Morgan patted the top of her head. Only her pride was injured. Not that she really had much to begin with.

"Bend your knees more!" Hannah called. "Like you're squatting on the board!"

Morgan got herself back into position, then gave the thumbs-up again. The boat started up slower this time, which helped. She managed not to flip over immediately, and she started to move forward, still squatting against the board. Then, as the boat picked up speed, she slowly and carefully straightened her legs, rotating the board so that it pointed forward.

She was doing it! She was actually wakeboarding like a proper Long Island girl!

She grinned at the boat, and she could just make out the cheers above the roar of the motor. The board vibrated beneath her, and the wind pulled at her hair as she zoomed along the surface of the sea. This wasn't so bad, really. Maybe it was even fun?

Then she hit the choppy wake and her board cut out from under her. She lost her grip on the rope and went flying.

Before she had time to take a breath, she smashed into the water so hard that she went under, even wearing the life jacket. She was surrounded by swirling darkness, so turned around that she didn't even know which way was up. *The sea is a cruel mistress.* Piper had warned her, but it was too late. Morgan's arms and legs flailed helplessly as her lungs screamed for air. It was just like her nightmare. Was she drowning? Was this how Joseph Klaus had felt? What if he had died right in this spot? They never recovered his body. It could be directly below her.

Then she felt something touch her foot.

She screamed and got a lungful of seawater, which filled her chest with a searing cold.

But a moment later, the life jacket finally did its job and hauled her flailing, panicked body back to the surface. The sun hit her face as she coughed and spat up seawater between gasps of air, her shoulders spasming.

She wasn't dead, but she'd lost the rope. She looked around, her eyes burning from the salt. There was nothing but open water surrounding her, and maybe a dead boy beneath her . . .

"Morgan!"

She craned her head around and saw the boat behind her. Everyone was calling to her, asking if she was okay. It took her a moment to decide if she actually was, then she patted her head.

"You want to go again?" called Ms. Witherspoon.

Morgan shook her head.

Tressa's mom turned the boat around and approached slowly, cutting the engine as she drew close. Morgan awkwardly pushed herself through the water over to the platform and pulled herself out.

"Don't worry about it," said Tressa. "We all fall at first."

"Yeah," chimed in Piper. "You did better than me the first time. You were really going for a minute there."

"Thanks . . ."

For once, Morgan wasn't that bothered about looking like a total fool in front of her new friends. Instead she stared out at the rippling water. It was still a vast and beautiful sparkling stretch of sea. But she was also now painfully aware of what might lie beneath.

Her thoughts drifted back to that yellowed newspaper clipping from nearly a hundred years ago:

LOCAL BOY BELIEVED DROWNED

Somewhere out in that expanse of water were the remains of Joseph Klaus, who had braved that cruel mistress to escape his Nazi summer camp. And he had died alone and terrified in its dark, watery depths.

INTERLUDE

Joseph didn't know how long he waited in the sweltering heat under the tarp in the back of the truck. He must have passed out, because he woke suddenly when the truck's engine revved to life.

It was dark and cool by then, so he knew it must be night. He wondered if anyone had noticed he still hadn't come back from the hike. If not, they would realize it when they went to his cot to drag him into the woods for another beating.

But none of that mattered anymore. Because the truck began to drive slowly through the gate and away from the camp, taking Joseph with it. Wherever he was headed, it would be better than what he was leaving behind.

The truck came to a stop about thirty minutes later. It occurred to Joseph that the driver might check the cargo, and if he discovered him, would certainly take him back to the camp. So before that could happen,

Joseph slipped out from under the tarp and jumped to the ground.

He looked around in the darkness, trying to get his bearings. It was clearly a shipyard, with several large sailing vessels on struts and a line of rowboats stacked on their sides. The place looked somewhat familiar, but he couldn't say for certain in the dim light of the moon. Directly in front of him and stretching off to one side, he saw the glittering dark of the sea. To the other side, he could make out a cluster of lights. A harbor town? Was it Port Jefferson? If so, his home should be directly across the water from where he stood.

He heard the truck door slam shut behind him, which meant the driver had gotten out. Joseph sprinted across the short stretch of sandy ground and hid behind the line of rowboats. Peeking between the boats, he watched as the driver removed one of the crates from the back of the truck and carried it over to the main building in the shipyard. Joseph had been right to flee the truck when he did.

Now he turned and looked longingly across the

harbor. He couldn't see it, but his home was nestled into the base of the hills on the far shore. He was so close, but he would have to walk all the way around the harbor—hugging the coast from the shipyard into town—then circle around and hike up one side of a steep hill and down the other.

How long would that take? Hours? What if one of the adults from the camp saw him as he was walking through town? He knew most of them didn't live at the camp. Also, the sky had grown an ominous purple. Dense clouds were gathering, and the wind was picking up. If it really began to storm, would he even be able to make it up the hill with all the mud?

Joseph sighed despairingly. He'd come so far . . .

Then his eyes fell upon a rowboat, and he got an idea.

It was stealing. He knew that was wrong. But he was so tired and miserable, half delirious from hunger, exhaustion, and probably dehydration. He just wanted to get home and into the embrace of his parents. Surely they wouldn't be mad that he ran away once he told them about the terrible things that had happened there. He could picture their concerned faces. He could hear their soothing words. Feel their gentle touch.

He just had to get home. Then everything would be okay again . . .

TWENTY-ONE

Morgan should have been happy. She'd finally made some friends. Every day at school they chatted before class, in between classes, at lunch, and after school. She was invited over to their houses for dinner. Hannah even started calling her by name instead of "new girl." It seemed like the Brooklyn girl had successfully acclimated to Long Island.

So why *wasn't* she happy? She kept thinking back to what Joel had said about Zophia Zye: *You realize that even though she's surrounded by all these generals and loyal soldiers, she's actually pretty lonely. None of them really see her.*

Not that Morgan thought she was anywhere as cool as the Night Queen, of course. But it was that same feeling of being alone in a crowd. She had friends, but she understood there were requirements to those friendships. She had to feign interest in whatever was going on with "Jake and them," the pack of athletic, cocksure boys that Hannah and the others acted like they didn't care about but were clearly obsessed with. She couldn't talk with these friends about the Night Queen books or any Japanese pop culture stuff. And she *definitely* couldn't mention creepy things like her increasing preoccupation with the ghost Nazi boy that she had vanquished from her house. And she *did* think about him. Possibly even more than when he'd been haunting her.

Joel would have understood, of course. But he'd asked her out and then she ghosted him. She wasn't sure what to do about that—and every day that she continued to ghost him only made it worse. Of course friends were supposed to advise one another on how to navigate boy issues, but she couldn't exactly ask Tressa or Hannah what she should do about the boy they had all dubbed the creepy weirdo.

So she couldn't talk about the three things that occupied most of her brain: Joseph Klaus, Joel Applebaum, and the Night Queen. Since she didn't know what else to talk about, she usually went along with what *they* were interested in, even though a lot of it didn't hold her attention.

Morgan often sat and smiled vaguely as the three longtime friends chattered on about whatever. Sometimes her mind drifted back to that moment when she'd genuinely thought a drowned ghost had touched her ankle in Long Island Sound. It had been a ridiculous idea. She knew that. Probably just some seaweed or even a fish. And yet, she still couldn't shake the memory of that bolt of terror. She had felt helplessness and panic in that dark, cold, deep water. Joseph Klaus had probably felt something similar at the moment of his death.

On Tuesday she tried to bring up these feelings with her new friends in a roundabout way. But she immediately regretted it.

They were at Piper's house, which Morgan was not surprised to learn was one of the beautiful Victorian-style homes with the wraparound porches. Like the other big fancy houses in Port Jefferson, Piper's was set at a much higher elevation. Morgan could see the entire harbor as they sat on the porch. Maybe that's what prompted her to say something.

"Do kids ever drown in the harbor?"

"What?" Hannah looked incredulously at her.

Piper frowned. "I sure hope not . . ."

"I feel like you hear more about people dying from *car accidents* than drownings," said Tressa.

"Oh . . ." Morgan already realized it had been a mistake to bring it up.

Tressa's eyes narrowed. "Kinda morbid question. You've got a gothy, emo streak in you, don't you, Morgan?"

"I mean, with my name I guess it was inevitable, right?" She grinned, trying to play it off.

"Huh?" said Hannah. "What do you mean 'with your name'?"

"You know, Morgan le Fay? King Arthur's witchy half-sister?"

All three of them stared at her, and it dawned on Morgan that in trying to deflect from one weird aspect of herself, she'd tripped over a different one. She'd always loved that her parents named her after such a dark and strange character of legend. Her friends back in Brooklyn, as well as her friends on the Night Queen chat server, had all agreed that it was very cool. But the looks she was getting now suggested her new friends did not think so. At all.

"*Who* now?" asked Hannah.

Thankfully, before Morgan could dig herself any deeper by explaining the twisted and extremely "gothy, emo" origins of the legendary Morgan le Fay, Piper's father came out with some snacks.

"Here you are, girls," he said cheerfully as he placed the tray of carrots, broccoli, celery, and dip on the small wicker table.

"Thanks, Mr. Morrison," Morgan said, although more for the distraction than the veggies.

"My pleasure." He gave her an anxious smile. It was the same smile Piper always gave, in fact. Maybe it was genetic?

While it was true that Morgan struggled to enjoy her newfound friend circle, she *did* find it interesting to go to all the different houses and meet the different families. Piper was an only child like Morgan. Her family's beautiful Victorian house was so neat and tidy that Morgan was afraid to touch anything. Her parents were also extremely pretty and extremely uptight, everything spoken behind tight smiles. They even used matching cloth napkins at dinner. Morgan's family used cloth napkins because it was better for the environment, but she didn't think there was a single matching pair among them.

On Wednesday, they went to Tressa's house for dinner, which was much more relaxed. Tressa and Hannah were next-door neighbors who lived on Jefferson Street, which was a little farther away from the water and not as fancy as Piper's street.

Tressa's father was a tall, round, jolly guy with a bald head and a bushy black beard that was shot through with streaks of gray. He made Morgan think of Santa Claus, and she even mentioned to Tressa that her father could be one of those Santas little kids go to at shopping centers.

Tressa gave her a look that was half amused, half incredulous. "A Black Santa?"

"Is that weird?" Morgan asked worriedly.

"Maybe not in Brooklyn . . ." said Tressa in a way that implied maybe it was Brooklyn that was weird. And by extension, perhaps Morgan as well.

In addition to the older sister at NYU, Tressa had two younger siblings: twin boys who seemed constantly on the verge of exploding into utter chaos and yet never did. Morgan couldn't decide if that was because of Ms. Witherspoon's calm command, Mr. Witherspoon's cheerful redirection, or Tressa's cool-big-sister influence. Maybe all three. It was a warm, boisterous home and Morgan felt very relaxed when she was there, even if it was a little louder than her own.

While Hannah's house was also loud, it was not at all warm—and definitely not relaxing. Morgan preferred even the polite stuffiness of Piper's house to the brusque indifference she found at the Meyer house on Thursday. It felt like everyone was either shouting or sullenly silent. Hannah's father worked late, so he wasn't there, and her mother seemed annoyed that Hannah had brought her friends over. Maybe because it was already pretty crowded. Even with Mr. Meyer gone, there was Hannah; her younger sister, Mia; Ms. Meyer; Grandma Meyer; and Great-Grandpa Meyer, all in a house only about as big as Morgan's. In fact, everyone in the family seemed irritated to even be in the same room with one another most of the time. None more so than Great-Grandpa Meyer. The old man never left the living room recliner, not even during dinner. Instead he sat in his plaid pants drinking whiskey and watching golf on television.

"Ignore him," was all Hannah said as they walked past.

It wasn't fun going to Hannah's house, but it helped Morgan understand her new friend better. Hannah might have some rough edges, but compared to the rest of her family, she was actually pretty nice.

CHAPTER · TWENTY-TWO

As nice as it was to gain some perspective about her new friends by having dinners at their homes, and as much as she did *not* enjoy her own parents' cooking, Morgan found herself unexpectedly pleased to be eating rubbery tofu and mushy pasta at her own house on Friday.

"Nice to see you, stranger," her father said once the three of them sat down. "Decided to grace us with your presence this evening?"

Morgan grinned. "You're welcome."

"I'm glad that all your hard work making friends has paid off," said her mother.

"Yeah . . ." Morgan hadn't thought of it that way, but she supposed it *had* paid off. At the cost of her friendship with Joel.

Almost as though reading her mind, her father asked, "How did that history project go?"

"Wh-what do you mean?" Since Morgan wasn't a great liar, she hoped her father wouldn't press her for details on the fake history project alibi.

"You were hanging out with that Joel boy all the time, and now suddenly you're not," said her father. "So I figured the project must be finished."

"Oh," she said. "Yeah. It's finished."

In a sense that was true. After all, she'd gotten rid of the ghost. It didn't *feel* finished, but that was probably because it had been a little anticlimactic.

"He seems like a nice boy," her mother said carefully. "Don't you think he'd get along with the girls?"

"Definitely not."

"Why not?" asked her father.

She couldn't tell her parents that the girls all called him a creepy weirdo, because they would think that was hurtful. Which of course it was, but she didn't want her parents to dislike her new friends.

"He's not into the same stuff as them" was all she said.

"Oh?" asked her mother. "What's he into?"

It occurred to Morgan that her parents were being uncharacteristically nosy about Joel.

"You guys know he's not my boyfriend or anything," she told them flatly.

Her parents exchanged a knowing expression, and Morgan realized with a sinking feeling she'd just fallen into their trap.

Her father smiled smugly. "Who said anything about *boyfriends*?"

"Gabe." Her mother gave him a stern, furrowed brow. Then she softened again as she turned back to Morgan. "Sweetie, you're reaching an age where social interactions start to get more . . . *complicated*. You may feel conflicting pressures coming from different directions, and that can be a hard thing to juggle."

"I guess a little . . ." admitted Morgan.

"It's okay to feel overwhelmed occasionally," said her mother. "It's normal, in fact."

"Social interactions *still* overwhelm me sometimes," her father admitted cheerfully.

Her mother gave him another hard look, but he just shrugged.

"It's the truth."

She sighed. "Yes, I suppose it is. Anyway, Morgan, we can both tell something is bothering you, but we won't push you any further. Right, Gabe?"

Another steely look at her father.

"Right," he said solemnly.

"You know we're always here if you want to talk about anything," her mother continued. "More importantly, we want you to know that we trust you, and that whatever is going on, it will work out, so long as you stay true to yourself."

She smiled at Morgan with such confidence that it almost hurt. Because Morgan had spent most of the week trying her best *not* to be herself. But she smiled anyway.

"Thanks, Mom."

The following day, Morgan's father sent her into town on an errand. Most of his art was digital, but sometimes he did hand-drawn commissions that needed to be mailed out. He hated going to the post office, and even though Morgan said she hated it too, it had somehow become *her* job to take art down to the post office.

"What do you think?" He held up the poster for her to see before packing it up.

Her eyes widened. "That's from *Carrion Flowers*, isn't it?"

"Oh, you know it?" he asked. "I'm not as up on anime stuff as you, obviously, but I watched a couple episodes so that I would know what I was getting into for this commission. It's intense stuff."

"I haven't watched it," she said quickly.

"No?" He seemed surprised. "It's pretty good. Reminds me a little of Gaiman's *Sandman*, actually."

"Well, it's TV-MA, so I'm not allowed."

"Oh, right . . . that's a rule we have . . ."

He always said it like that when it was a rule her mother had made. Sometimes he just agreed because it wasn't worth arguing about. Morgan knew this because there was often an eye roll that went along with it.

"Anyway," he said as he furled the poster and slid it into a cardboard tube, "take this down to the post office and I'll treat you."

"To what?" she asked as she took the tube.

"A bright shiny nickel?" he asked hopefully.

She gave him a withering look.

"Okay, okay. It was worth a try," he said. "So what, then? Another Night Queen portrait?"

She hesitated for a moment, then surprised herself by asking, "Can you do Bianca Gray from *Infamous Motley*?"

"Really?" He looked surprised as well. "That was the one about the supervillain girl with the commedia dell'arte mask, right? Sure, that'll be fun, actually."

Morgan's eyes narrowed. "Are you saying drawing the Night Queen isn't fun?"

"I mean . . ." He gave her a pained smile. "The first time was fun, but it does get a little old always drawing the same person."

"I bet you wouldn't say that if you were drawing the Sandman."

"True," he admitted.

As Morgan carried the cardboard tube down to the post office, she wondered why she'd asked for an *Infamous Motley* sketch. If she wanted to make up with Joel, it would probably be a good apology present. Was that the reason? She hadn't been consciously planning to do that, but she couldn't deny that that the idea made her feel better about having ghosted him. And yet, even *with* an apology present in hand, she knew it would be super awkward, not to mention dangerous for her social life . . .

She was still mulling this over as she entered the post office. Like everything else on Long Island, it was much more spacious than her old post office in Brooklyn.

"Oh, Morgan!"

She turned at the sound of her name and saw the bright red face of Professor Johnson grinning at her.

"Hey, Professor," she said.

"Are you still working on your history project?" he asked.

"Oh, I, uh, think it's finished."

"Ah, what a shame," he said. "I should have thought to tell you this when you came to visit, then. But it only occurred to me later that you could have included first-person testimony about Camp Siegfried in your project."

"What do you mean?"

"Old Ernst Meyer over on Jefferson Street actually *attended* the camp as a boy."

Morgan's eyes widened. "You said *Meyer*? On *Jefferson* Street?"

Johnson's bushy white eyebrows rose. "Do you know him?"

She recalled the grim old man in plaid pants at Hannah's house and shivered.

"I think he might be my friend's great-grandfather."

CHAPTER

TWENTY-THREE

Morgan didn't have to go home right after she mailed the package, so she wandered aimlessly around town for a while. More than ever, she wanted to talk to someone about Joseph Klaus, but the only person she could ask was Joel, who she wasn't talking to. It was the same conflict she'd felt all week, and now it was so strong that it occupied her entire brain. She needed space to think, and although she loved her father, he did not always give her that.

This could be it. If Great-Grandpa Meyer had known Joseph, maybe he could answer all her lingering questions. What had Joseph been like? What happened to him at that camp? What had been so bad that it had driven him to such a dangerous undertaking? And what, in the end, had the ghost wanted before Morgan drove it away? Maybe if she learned at least *some* of those things, she would stop obsessing.

And yet, there were so many reasons *not* to talk to the old man. First and foremost, he was terrifying. Second, in order to see him, she would need to ask Hannah if she could, and that would mean she'd have to tell Hannah about the whole ghost Nazi thing. Well, maybe not the ghost part, but definitely the Nazi part. And that could completely ruin whatever small progress she'd made in the friends department.

Was it worth all of that? It was only an obsession after all. Just something she was into, like the Night Queen series, except not even as famous. It wasn't like there was a Camp Siegfried chat server, or a trending #CampSiegfried hashtag. Other than a few blog posts and a Wikipedia article, she'd hardly found anything about it online. Even most of the people who lived in the area didn't seem to know about it.

Nobody else cared. So maybe she should just let it go . . .

Morgan wandered down Main Street to the shoreline, then through the grassy park along the water. Eventually she came across a small playground. Thoughts still spinning in her head, she sat down on a swing.

She could see the entire harbor from that spot. Nearby was the big ferry terminal that had helped make Port Jefferson so popular, although there wasn't currently a ship at the dock. Off to one side of the harbor was a massive shipyard, with all kinds of boats set up on struts for repair. On the other side of the harbor, she knew, was her house, although the uneven coastline prevented her from seeing it from where she sat.

Joseph Klaus had died trying to row across that stretch of water. In the dark, terrified and alone during a storm.

Morgan sighed and closed her eyes. There she went again. Obsessed over a Nazi ghost boy who didn't matter to anyone but her.

When she opened her eyes, she found herself looking at one of the swing set's poles.

Etched into the metal was a Nazi swastika. It looked quite new.

Her stomach squirmed as she stared at it. She tried to scuff the symbol with her shoe, but it didn't fade at all. It was still there. Still awful. Because someone had put it there, not eighty-some years ago, but *recently*.

Morgan remembered how badly Joel had wanted to visit Yaphank. She could still picture his pale, tense face when he'd suggested the idea.

That's when she understood that she was *not* the only one who cared. And as long as swastikas were still being carved into playgrounds, what happened to Joseph Klaus mattered a whole lot.

CHAPTER

TWENTY-FOUR

When Morgan knocked on Hannah's door, Ms. Meyer answered.

"Hi, Ms. Meyer, is—"

Before Morgan could finish, Ms. Meyer turned and shouted, "Hannah! One of your little friends is at the door!"

"My friends are not little!" she heard Hannah shout back.

"They're all little to me!" retorted Ms. Meyer.

Then she walked off, leaving Morgan standing there in front of the open door. A lifetime of her parents' upbringing would not allow her to enter without permission, so she waited until eventually Hannah appeared.

"Oh, hey." She seemed surprised to see Morgan. Or maybe surprised to see anyone voluntarily visit her home. "What's up?"

Morgan knew her friend well enough by then to understand that she should just cut to the chase. "I have a favor to ask."

Hannah's eyes narrowed suspiciously. "Let's hear it."

"I need to talk to your great-grandpa."

Hannah clearly hadn't been expecting *that* to be the favor. "What? Why?"

"W-Well, it's sort of complicated, but—"

Hannah held up her hand. "You know what? Never mind. I don't actually care. Talk to him all you want. It'll probably be the most exciting thing he's done in years. And it's early enough in the day that he won't be so drunk he shouts curses at you the whole time. Probably."

"Oh . . ." Morgan hadn't expected it to be this easy. "Thanks."

Hannah gestured for her to enter. "You know where to find him."

Morgan tried to swallow her nervousness as she entered a house that hadn't felt particularly welcoming before, and now seemed heavy with a quiet menace. The front door opened into a small foyer, with the living room off to the left. She could see the old man sitting there in the dark room, illuminated only by the televised golf match. He was a small figure, with wispy white hair that didn't cover much of his spotted scalp. He was hunched forward, and Morgan couldn't tell if he was glaring at the screen or if that was just his face.

She tried to tell herself that he was just an old man who couldn't actually harm her, but it didn't do much good. It took several deep breaths before she mustered up the courage to enter the room.

Hannah had claimed not to care, but she followed behind Morgan and stood just inside the doorway, leaning against the wall. Was she curious after all? Or was she more concerned for Morgan? Either way, Morgan found to her surprise that she was grateful for her friend's presence. It was what finally gave her the courage to speak.

"Mr. Meyer?"

The old man didn't respond. Maybe he was hard of hearing? Or maybe he was ignoring her on purpose.

"Mr. Meyer, s-sorry to disturb you," Morgan said a little louder, "but I wanted to ask if you knew Joseph Klaus."

There was a dreadfully long pause, with only the quiet murmur of the golf broadcast announcer in the background.

Finally the old man picked up the TV remote and turned off the golf. The room was now lit only by the feeble sunlight streaming in through the partly closed window shades.

He slowly rotated his chair to face her. She was stunned to see tears in his bleary eyes, though his face looked as stern and grim as ever.

"I always thought this day would come," he said in a thin, raspy voice. "But I did not expect the question to be asked by the likes of you."

"I, uh, live at his old house," she said. "And I . . . found his uniform."

His wrinkled face creased up even further, as though the news caused him physical pain.

"Ah."

Morgan waited for several moments, but when he didn't say anything more, she asked, "So . . . you *did* know him?"

"Not well, but . . ." The tears came springing back to his eyes as his voice tightened up.

Morgan glanced at Hannah. Was she mad that Morgan had made her great-grandfather cry? But her friend only stared in wide-eyed amazement, like she had never imagined such a thing was even possible.

"We called him 'die heulsuse,'" Mr. Meyer said quietly as he stared down into his glass of whiskey. "The crybaby. We told ourselves we were doing it for his own good."

Morgan waited a few moments, but when it seemed like he might not go on, she asked, "What did you do?"

"We beat him, of course," the old man said flatly. "Every night. For nearly a week. We convinced ourselves that it would make him strong. Like us. But we were wrong. We were weak, and he was the strong one. Because he refused to let . . . *them* turn him into something else."

"The Nazis?" asked Morgan as gently as she could.

He nodded. "We never imagined it would end like it did. First the counselor, Tillie Koch, died. Then Joseph. And even after that, we still didn't understand that they had been the bravest among us. It took me many years to grasp that, and even longer to accept it. Perhaps if even one more of us had the courage to resist like Joseph, both their lives might have been saved. Yet the world is made terrible not by evil men, but by the cowardice of those who follow them."

CHAPTER

TWENTY-FIVE

Mr. Meyer said no more after that. He only sat there in his chair in the darkness, staring down into his glass, now empty except for a few half-melted ice cubes.

Eventually Morgan left, and Hannah followed her. Once they reached the front door, however, Hannah blocked her path.

"Okay, what . . . was that?" demanded Hannah.

"Sorry," said Morgan. "I didn't realize he'd get so upset."

"I don't care about that," said Hannah. "The guy just said more to you in five minutes than he's said to me in five *years*! Who was this Joseph kid you were talking about?"

"He's the reason everyone thinks my house is haunted," said Morgan. "He drowned in the harbor back during the 1930s after running away from his summer camp. And I found this kid-sized Nazi uniform in our attic. It turns out the camp, which your great-grandpa also went to, was, like, a Nazi training camp about twelve miles from here."

"You're saying my great-grandpa was a Nazi?" asked Hannah.

"No!" Morgan said quickly. "He was just one of the kids sent to this camp. I think he was probably as much a victim as Joseph."

"Sure didn't sound like it," said Hannah. "You heard what he was saying. Seems like he fit right in with them."

"Yeah, but . . . he was just a kid, you know?" Morgan said. "Everyone around him was telling him that he should act a certain way. How many of us could really stand up against all that pressure when we're alone?"

"Nah, forget that," said Hannah. "Morgan, you're way

too nice. The way I see it, if a person can't be them-selves, then who even are they?"

Morgan stared at her for a moment as understanding finally dawned. It was exactly what her mother had said. That everything would work out *if* she was true to herself. Because as Hannah had just pointed out, if she wasn't herself, who even was she?

"You're totally right," she told Hannah.

Her friend shrugged. "Obviously."

"I have to tell Joel about this." Morgan pushed past her and stepped through the doorway.

"Wait," Hannah called. "*Creepy weirdo* Joel?"

"No," said Morgan. "*My friend* Joel."

CHAPTER TWENTY-SIX

Morgan was tempted to just rush right over to Joel's house, but she knew she couldn't brush off how she'd been treating him. She had to make things right first. So she went home and made preparations.

The following morning, she knocked on Joel's door, a poster tube clutched in her hand. A middle-aged woman with curly black hair like Joel's answered the door.

"Can I help you?" she asked—a lot more politely than Ms. Meyer had.

"Hi, Ms. Applebaum. My name is Morgan Calvino. I live down the street."

"Oh, it's nice to finally meet you. I've heard so much about you."

"You have?" Morgan hadn't expected this, although she supposed Joel probably *would* have talked about her. Hopefully not too resentfully . . .

"Your father, Gabe, introduced himself a few days back. He said he was glad Joel was your first friend in Port Jeff and that it really seemed to help you adjust."

"Right . . ." said Morgan.

"Not that my own son tells me any of this." Ms. Applebaum sighed. "Boys, right? Well, hopefully Joel will grow up to be a nice man like your father."

"S-Sure?" Morgan had never heard anyone say they hoped their son would grow up to be like her dad. Frankly she couldn't imagine anyone else like her father.

"Anyway, I'm sure you're here for Joel. You want to come in?"

"Thanks."

Ms. Applebaum ushered her into a house that looked very much like her own.

"Wait here, I'll go pry him away from his computer."

Morgan stood in the foyer, feeling her nervousness grow. She clenched the cardboard tube and waited.

She heard heavy footsteps come down the stairs and a moment later Joel appeared. His expression was confused and guarded, but not full of hatred. So that was good.

"Hey," he said.

"Hey," she said.

They stood awkwardly for a moment as Morgan struggled to figure out how best to begin. Ultimately she decided on bribery, and thrust the tube at him.

"This is for you."

He hesitated a moment, then took it and uncapped the tube. He slid the rolled poster out and unfurled it. Then his eyes went wide.

The image was of Bianca Gray, the protagonist of the popular anime and manga series *Infamous Motley*. In the story, she was the daughter of a well-known super-villain who had been raised to be his successor, although she didn't really want to be a villain. But when her father was apprehended by police, there was this huge twist in the story because Bianca realized that her father wasn't actually a villain. He was a freedom fighter, and the country in which they lived was a fascist authoritarian state. In order to rescue her father, she assumed the "supervillain" identity of Motley, donning an old commedia dell'arte half mask.

In the image Morgan's father had drawn, Bianca was dressed as Motley, complete with goofy Columbina mask and multicolored cropped leather jacket. Motley was famous for her ridiculous acrobatics, so she was upside down in the image, standing on one hand. She appeared to be about to kick the viewer. There was a word balloon coming from her mouth that said, *"Hey, Joel! Sorry I been bad!"*

It didn't exactly fit with the image because why would she be apologizing when she was about to kick someone? But Morgan had asked her dad to add it later, after he'd already done most of the work. She'd wanted something that made it clear this was an apology gift for Joel, while also trying to remain true to the spirit of his favorite anime character, who would have made it into a cheeky one-liner.

"You drew this?" Joel asked in awe as he stared at the picture.

She shook her head. "No, I asked my dad to do it. He draws comics and stuff. But I mean it about being sorry. I shouldn't have ghosted you like that."

"Oh." He looked at her for a moment, then looked away. "It's okay. I get it. I crossed a line."

This confirmed that he *had* in fact been asking her on a date. She had no idea how she felt about that at all, but she didn't want to get sidetracked now that she'd worked her way up to a reconciliation.

"I'm not sure if you did or not," she admitted. "But it kind of freaked me out. I don't know how I *should* have handled things, although ghosting you wasn't it. Because I know how it feels to be ignored by someone you thought was a friend. So I'm sorry."

They stood there awkwardly again.

"Thanks," he said at last as he carefully rolled the poster up and slid it back into the tube.

"So . . . are we good?" Morgan asked.

"Of course," he said calmly.

Either he hadn't been as upset about the whole thing as she'd thought, or she had really nailed the apology gift. Or maybe this was just how boys were.

"Great, so you want to go to Yaphank with me?"

He tilted his head, his mouth quirked in surprise. "Really? When?"

"How about right now?" she asked. "My mom said she'd take us, and Sundays are her only proper day off."

TWENTY-SEVEN

The drive to Yaphank only took about half an hour, but it was probably the most excruciating thirty minutes Morgan had ever experienced because her mom spent the entire drive interrogating Joel. Morgan suspected the opportunity to question him might have been the only reason her mom agreed to drive them in the first place.

"So, Joel, have you lived out on Long Island your whole life?"

"Yes, Ms. Zeggini."

Morgan's mother hadn't changed her last name when

her parents got married, but Morgan had filled Joel in on that. Fortunately he'd remembered.

"And your parents?"

She was interrogating him as only a lawyer could. But he seemed happy to answer any questions she posed with honesty.

"Oh, the Applebaums have been on Long Island a long time. In fact, my great-great-grandfather apparently ran a big bootlegging operation back in the 1920s. My mom says we're not supposed to talk about that part of the family history, but I think it's pretty cool. He was like the Jewish Al Capone of Long Island."

Maybe a little too much honesty.

"So you think being a gangster is cool?" Morgan's mother asked in a scarily neutral tone. "Is that what you want to do with your life?"

"Oh, no, Ms. Zeggini," he said quickly. "I just think it's interesting from a historical perspective. I'm going to be a writer, you see."

"A writer, huh?" her mother asked, voice still unnervingly neutral. "And what will you to do to *earn a living?*"

He laughed. "Good one, Ms. Zeggini."

Morgan knew her mother had not been joking.

Finally they arrived in Yaphank. Morgan never thought she'd be so relieved to get to a former Nazi summer camp. Although it wasn't at all what she expected.

"You're sure this is the place?" she asked Joel.

They'd turned off the main road, down a narrow side street with small, fenced-in houses on either side, then along an even narrower road lined by tall trees. Finally they came to an old weathered wooden sign that said GERMAN GARDENS.

"This is the place," said Joel. "After the war broke out, the camp was shut down. But it was still owned by a company called the German American Settlement League, which had been a front organization for the German American Bund, who were definitely Nazi fans. After the war, the same group turned it into a private residential community."

"I thought you said you were finished with this history project," said her mother.

Fortunately, Morgan had anticipated this question. "Our teacher offered extra credit. And you said I should always take extra credit assignments, even if I don't need them."

Her mother squinted her eyes doubtfully. She looked like she *wanted* to believe her daughter was dutifully following her advice, but couldn't quite convince herself of it. Still, she chose not to argue.

"So what will you do now?"

"Can you wait here while we look around?" Morgan asked.

"Don't go trespassing on people's property," said her mother.

"We won't, Ms. Zeggini," Joel promised.

Maybe *his* promises carried more weight than Morgan's, because that seemed to convince her. "All right. I'll stay here. Don't take too long."

They climbed out of the car and walked past the GERMAN GARDENS sign. On the other side it looked like any other middle-class suburb, with one- and two-level homes, fenced-in lawns, and small gardens. There were no sidewalks, so they walked slowly along the side of the road past house after house.

"Kinda weird, huh?" murmured Joel.

"Yeah," said Morgan. "Like, if you didn't know what had happened here, it could be anyplace."

"No more swastika shrubs or masonwork," pointed out Joel.

"No Adolf Hitler Street either," said Morgan. Now it was just German Boulevard.

"It's almost like the bad stuff never happened," said Joel. "Like it's been erased. Which makes it even creepier."

They continued to walk along the road. It was a beautiful, sunny fall afternoon. Some people were out, gardening or washing their cars in their driveways. Morgan wondered if any of them knew what had happened here.

When they crossed an intersection, Morgan glanced down the side street and saw more of the same. It wasn't fancy, but German Gardens seemed nice. Well, except . . .

"Geez, is it my imagination, or does everyone kind of look the same?" said Morgan. "I don't think I've seen a single Black person."

"I mean . . . until 2015, you had to be of German descent to live here."

"Is that even legal?" asked Morgan.

Joel shrugged. "I guess it's not actually that uncommon. Or it wasn't. Some of that stuff has been changing, but not as long ago as you'd expect."

After knowing that, the suburban community took on a less cheery demeanor for Morgan. And that was before she saw the house.

She stopped in her tracks. "Joel . . ."

He looked around. "What is it?"

She didn't want to point, in case someone was watching them, so she tilted her head. "Do you see that house?"

He followed the direction she was looking. He stared at it a moment, then asked, "What about it?"

"It's missing the swastika over the door, but other than that, it looks *exactly* like the ones in the pictures of Camp Siegfried."

"Oh . . ." he said. "Yeah, you're right."

"You know what that means?"

"It was built by forced child labor," he said.

"By kids like Joseph Klaus," she said.

He nodded.

"Do you think the people who live there *know*?" She wasn't sure why, but she suddenly felt so angry that her hands were shaking. "Do they know how much the people who built their house *suffered*? Would it even *matter* to them if they did?"

"They probably don't know," Joel assured her.

"Maybe I should tell them."

She would have done it too. Marched right up to that house, knocked on the door, and told whoever answered that crimes had been perpetrated while constructing their home. But Joel stopped her.

"You can't do that," he told her. "First, we don't know anything about these people. Maybe they're in a difficult situation of their own right now. How is learning that their home, the one place they feel safe, was built on cruelty going to make anything better for anyone? Or, they could be dangerous white supremacists who would not only be fine with forced child labor, but also shooting a nice Jewish boy who came to their house uninvited. We just have no idea. And lastly we promised your mom we wouldn't do anything."

"You're afraid of my mother," Morgan accused him.

"I am absolutely afraid of your mother," he said without a trace of embarrassment. "The point is . . . well, what *is* the point? What are we trying to do here?"

Morgan was silent for a moment. "Do you know who Tillie Koch was?"

Joel shook his head.

"Hannah's great-grandpa mentioned her, so I looked her up last night. She was a camp counselor who died. *Right here*." She glared at the ground beneath her feet, like it was somehow partly to blame. "The camp tried to make her out to be some big Nazi hero, but she wasn't. She was only a teenager trying to help some other kids and she *died*. And I just . . . I want someone to recognize that. I want it to *mean* something, you know?"

The two of them stood there, on the side of a suburban road next to a small house with a chain-link fence and a neatly trimmed lawn on a beautiful fall day, and all Morgan could think of was the pain and suffering that had been inflicted there. She wondered how many places were like this in America, constructed by children or slaves or Indigenous Americans, none of whom were able to enjoy it. Like it or not, that was part of America's history. Nice places built from cruelty.

Finally Joel gently said, "*We* recognize it. It means something to *us*. I don't know if there's anything more we can do. And maybe that's the point. Maybe that's what this whole thing was about. So that we could get to this place, in this moment, and understand that it's up to each of us to know these things. And to make sure they don't happen again."

Morgan looked at him for a moment, then nodded.

"You ready to head back?" he asked.

She nodded again.

They walked slowly the way they'd come, side by side.

The drive home was subdued. Morgan's mother seemed to catch the mood immediately and didn't continue her inquisition. All she asked was:

"Did you find what you were looking for?"

"Yeah," said Morgan. "I guess we did."

And perhaps that was true. Ultimately she'd been looking for some kind of end to all this. Some closure. And it did feel now like they'd gone about as far as they could go. She no longer felt that burning obsession to *learn more* now. Maybe she'd left that in Yaphank.

Unfortunately she also brought something back with her.

Or rather, some*one*.

INTERLUDE

Joseph Klaus had some experience rowing, so he knew how it was done. You had to face away from where you wanted to go, toward the stern of the small boat. You had to find a rhythm so that both arms were pulling at the same time, otherwise you'd be moving in zigzags, or worse, in circles. He'd done it bunches of times. But never this far. Never at night. And definitely never during a storm.

It began okay. Sure, he was so tired his vision kept blurring, so hungry that he felt light-headed, and so thirsty that he was tempted to drink seawater even though he knew it would make him sick. But he was so close to home now. Just on the other side of the harbor. The nightmare was nearly over.

He was about a quarter of the way across when the wind began to pick up. The stars in the purple sky overhead disappeared, snuffed out by dark, seething clouds. The gray water that surrounded him rippled in the wind like a bed of spikes. His little boat rocked so hard it became difficult to steer.

Then the rain began to fall, stippling the spiky gray water. Before he set out, he'd pulled off his Nazi uniform in a fit of defiance and left it back on the shore. Now he regretted that impulsive act as the downpour soaked through his thin undergarments and chilled him to the bone. But he was halfway home. There was no turning back.

The storm grew stronger and the ripples turned to waves, shoving his little boat up and down as it moved from one rise to the next. Then a wave lifted him so high that his oars flailed helplessly, unable to reach the water on either side. He braced himself for the drop back down, but it hit so hard, it rattled his jaw.

He was still recovering from the impact when another wave curled over the boat and crashed into him, knocking him over the side. He managed to grab the rail, and thankfully the boat didn't flip over as he clambered back in.

Then he realized that he'd lost one of the oars.

He looked desperately around the boat to see if there

was a spare, but the only things in it were what he'd taken from the shipyard. He hadn't thought to pack a spare oar.

Well, he still had one oar left. It would have to do. He paddled the rowboat like it was a canoe, first on one side, then the other. All the while, torrents of water hammered down on his head, shoulders, and back.

A flash of light temporarily blinded him, followed by the sharp detonation of thunder. He blinked back the spots in his vision, searching for the far shore. But the rain was falling so hard now that he couldn't see more than ten feet in any direction. He couldn't use the town lights as a fixed navigational point—or the moon, or *anything*. For all he knew, he'd been knocked off course and was now desperately rowing out to sea . . .

But he couldn't just sit there bobbing among the frothing waves while his boat slowly filled with rainwater. He had to keep moving or he would never get home.

So he paddled against the churning, hungry current, his thin arms taut, his jaw clenched to keep his teeth from chattering. The boat rocked continuously, threatening to capsize at any moment, but still he pressed on. He had to get home. Once he got home everything would be fine.

Another wave crashed across the bow, knocking his remaining oar out of his hand. He reached desperately for it. If he lost that oar, he was finished. But as he leaned over, tilting the boat diagonally on its side, another wave smacked into the hull and flipped it over.

The gunwale slammed into Joseph's head as he hit the water, sending him plunging downward. He struggled to reach the surface, but his head ached, and the current pulled at his legs like invisible hands, dragging him down even farther . . .

It was dark and he could see nothing.

It was cold and he could feel nothing.

He was so tired.

So miserable.

But he had to get home.

Then everything would be fine.

He just had to . . .

Get home

Get Home

GET

HOME

CHAPTER

TWENTY-EIGHT

It was night by the time Morgan and her mother dropped Joel off at his house and headed home. It had been a long day and Morgan was ready to curl up with a can of coconut seltzer and dive into volume eight of *My Secret Dream of a Boring Life.*

By the beginning of volume eight, the misunderstanding between Zophia Zye and Kosuke had been resolved. And just in time, because the undead kingdom of Nezhit decided to invade the Night Queen's domain. The last three volumes of the series were about this all-out war between the two most powerful nations in the world. It had vast, exciting battles, and ridiculously overpowered magic fights between the Night Queen's forces and the evil undead royalty of Nezhit.

That was all great fun. But what Morgan loved most about this last plot arc was that it was basically one big reward for all the deep relationships that had slowly formed over the previous seven books under Zophia Zye's guidance. Whenever it seemed that the Night Queen's forces were about to lose, two people, usually a human and a nonhuman, came together and, thanks to the strong bonds they'd developed, they were able to work together to save the day. *Some* fans complained that it got a little predictable after a while, but Morgan didn't care. She loved it every single time.

Morgan sighed happily as she pulled volume eight from the bookshelf and plopped down on her bed. She gazed at the cover for a few moments. This one had Zophia Zye—as always in her high-collared black cape and gown, blue skin, and jagged white hair. She looked extra fierce as she faced off against the cruel King Srogi, who wore black robes and a shiny steel mask so that all you could see were his glowing red eyes. It wasn't revealed what kind of undead Srogi was until volume nine. When Morgan first read the series, she'd assumed he was a vampire like Vladja, but he turned out to be something far worse. For this volume, however, that was still a mystery.

She opened the book to chapter one and was just about to begin reading. But she heard her mother let out an irritated groan from down the hall.

"You have got to be *kidding* me . . ." her mother grumbled. Then more loudly, "Morgan, go tell your dad the plumbing is screwed up again!"

Morgan's blood chilled. It couldn't be. That was all done now. Right?

"Wh-what do you mean it's screwed up?" she called.

"It's all dirty and gross again. Go tell your dad his whole 'It'll work itself out' plan was a bust after all. And have him call a plumber."

"O-Okay . . ." Morgan padded quietly downstairs, unease prickling her skin. Had the smudging worn off? Was it something she would have to do regularly? What if her parents wouldn't let her?

"Dad?" she called once she reached the bottom of the stairs.

"In here," he called from the kitchen. His voice sounded uncharacteristically grumpy.

"Dad, Mom said—"

"Let me guess, the plumbing is acting up again?" he asked testily.

She found him scowling at the kitchen sink.

"Yeah, how'd you . . . ?"

Then she saw that the sink was filled with seawater.

"It wouldn't stop coming out even after I turned it off," he said. "I had to shut off the water completely. Whatever's going on, it's affecting the whole house now."

He rubbed his bald head vigorously. That's what he did when he was especially stressed out. Morgan hated to see him like this.

"It's fine," he said at last, sounding only slightly less irritated. "I'll run out for some jugs of water for drinking and brushing teeth, and then I'll call a plumber first thing in the morning."

"You really think a plumber can fix this?" she asked.

"How would *I* know, Morgan?!" he snapped. Then he took a deep breath and gave her an apologetic smile. "Sorry, honey. This is just really stressful. Your mom and I have never owned a home before. Back in Brooklyn, this would have been the moment I'd be yelling at the landlord over the phone to come fix it. But now it's *our* responsibility, and we're kind of making it up as we go."

"I understand, Dad." She understood that trying to convince him they probably needed an exorcist rather than a plumber would only stress him out more.

He smiled gratefully. "It's nothing you need to worry about, honey. Your mom and I will sort it out. We're a heck of a team, after all."

"You sure are," she said, mostly to make him feel better. It seemed to work.

"Okay, first things first." He pushed up his sleeves and looked at the sink with new determination. "Let's drain this basin!"

Morgan went back to her room, a heavy dread growing in the pit of her stomach. She'd honestly thought the haunting was over. Had something triggered the ghost's return? It didn't seem like a coincidence that this was happening the same day they went to Yaphank.

She glanced at her bedroom window, which was closed. She walked over and yanked it up. What she heard was not the quiet, heartbroken sobs of a couple weeks ago. She wasn't even sure it was crying anymore. Instead it was more like a wail—desperate, ragged, and *angry*.

"Geez, is there a cat fight out there?" her mother called from her bedroom.

"Yeah," Morgan said tonelessly. "Cat fight."

She slid the window closed, which blocked out the furious screams of Joseph Klaus's ghost. But what did that matter? He was back, maybe worse than before. What could she do? When would it end?

She fell into her bed, unable to muster up the energy to read, or even change into her pajamas. She felt incredibly tired. Sick. Defeated.

It was only eight o'clock, but she turned off the light. And even in slumber she couldn't escape the ghost. Her dreams were filled with dark, churning water. She flailed in a cold and lightless world, not knowing where to go or which way was up. Her chest burned with the need to breathe, but she knew that the moment she did, her lungs would fill with seawater.

She clenched her teeth to stop herself, but her chest kept heaving, heaving.

Breathe! her body screamed at her. *You must breathe now!*

She awoke as a font of seawater gushed from her mouth, drenching her pillow.

Morgan scooted back onto her haunches, coughing and shaking. Tears rolled down her cheeks. Her stomach heaved, but nothing more came out.

Then she felt something on the back of her tongue. Reluctantly she reached into her mouth and felt a wide, slimy ribbon of seaweed. She slowly pulled and her stomach convulsed as the long, wet strip slid up her throat. At last it came free, wet and repellent as it gleamed in the moonlight that streamed through her window.

Her stomach heaved again, and she dashed to the bathroom, making it to the toilet just in time. She wretched so violently, her rib cage hurt. Tears streamed from her eyes, and she gasped for air.

Her mouth tasted of bile and gritty seawater, but the sink still wasn't working. So she staggered through the unlit house down to the kitchen. It would have been scary if she hadn't been so desperate to get the horrible taste out of her mouth.

Finally she reached the refrigerator and yanked it open. Her dad had bought several gallon jugs of water. Morgan ripped the lid off one and chugged straight from the jug. She stopped long enough to catch her breath, then did it again. She'd drunk half the jug before she could no longer taste the vomit and foul dark water from her dreams.

She'd been right. The ghost wasn't merely back. It was worse. Why? Was it making up for lost time? Or had she done something to upset it?

Her parents didn't let her keep her phone in her bedroom at night because they said it would lead to bad habits. So it charged overnight on the kitchen counter instead. She grabbed it now and started typing a message to Joel as she walked back upstairs.

> I dont know why but the ghost
> is back and it is mad

She jammed her thumb on the send button, then stood in the hallway for a moment, trying to calm herself down. She knew Joel wouldn't see the message until the morning, but sending it made her feel a tiny bit better.

Then it dawned on her that she was standing next to the balcony door. Her arm hairs prickled. Without meaning to, she turned her head toward the glass and looked into the blackness of night.

She saw it:

A pale, bloated face, flesh puckered with decay, staring at her with empty eye sockets, ragged mouth yawning hungrily.

Then it was gone.

CHAPTER

TWENTY-NINE

Morgan didn't sleep the rest of that night. Instead she lay on her bed and stared up at the ceiling as morning light slowly crept into her room. When her alarm went off, she dragged herself out of bed, her head a strange combination of fuzzy and keyed up.

Rather than reply to her text, Joel came out to meet her as she walked past his house on her way to school.

"Are you okay?" His face was creased with concern.

She tried to muster a smile but couldn't quite get there. "Honestly? Not really."

Her throat still felt a little scratchy and sore.

"You think this has something to do with us going to Yaphank yesterday?" he asked.

"It can't be a coincidence," she said. "I didn't sleep much last night, so I've been wondering: What happens to a ghost when you smudge them? I didn't even think about that when I did it. I just told the ghost to go away. But go away where? Maybe I accidentally sent it to the place where Camp Siegfried used to be."

"To the place it died trying to escape," said Joel. "No wonder it's so mad."

"Yeah." Was it bizarre that even after the awful night Morgan had, she felt guilty?

"Morgan, I'm so sorry," said Joel, his head bowed.

"Huh? Why?"

"It was my idea to go to Yaphank. If we'd just let it alone, maybe you wouldn't be going through all this."

She shook her head. "I wanted to go too. I . . . *needed* to go, I guess. And being there *meant* something to me. It felt important in a way that most things don't. Didn't you feel that way?"

"Yeah, I did," he admitted. "So what are we going to do now?"

"Well, it's never really haunted me during the day, so I think I'll be fine until tonight. After school I'm going to go talk to the woman at that Goddess by the Sea place. When I went there before, she'd said, 'a smudge stick to start,' which sounds like she might know more extreme methods to deal with ghosts if we need them."

He nodded. "Just . . . be careful today, okay?"

Morgan wondered what would have happened if she hadn't woken up and coughed up all that seawater when she did. Could she have drowned in her sleep last night? She shivered.

"I will," she promised.

As Morgan walked to school, the sky was a slate gray, and there was hardly any wind. It felt as if the whole world was holding its breath. For what? She didn't know.

She could barely pay attention during her morning classes. And when she joined her friends at lunch, her mind was so fixed on ghosts that she didn't even notice they were all giving her a strange look.

"So . . ." said Tressa. "You and Joel Applebaum, huh?"

Right. Morgan had finally admitted to Hannah that

Joel was her friend. But she did not have the time or energy for silly drama right now. She had *real* problems.

"Yeah. Me and Joel." She glared first at Tressa, and then at the other two girls. They all seemed taken aback by her sudden bluntness. "Joel might have been annoying when you all were little, but we're not kids anymore. Maybe if you actually gave him a chance, you'd see that he's a really nice guy."

"Okay, okay, chill." Tressa held up her hands. "If you say he's cool, I believe you."

"Oh, he's definitely *not* cool," said Morgan. "In fact, he's a huge anime dork. But that's the thing—so am I. I've been keeping a lid on it since we met because I didn't want you to think of me as a 'creepy weirdo' like him. But on Saturday, Hannah made me realize that if I can't be myself around people, then they don't really know me. And you can't be friends with someone you don't really know. So I'm done pretending to be something other than what I am. If that means I'm a creepy weirdo too, fine. My dad's also a weirdo, so I come by it honestly."

Now it was Tressa's turn to look annoyed. "Um, you

do realize I'm like the biggest *Ace of Bases* fan on the planet, right? So don't go making assumptions about people."

Morgan stared at her. *Ace of Bases* was a long-running sports manga and anime. It was about a group of Japanese juvenile delinquents who learn to get along and become productive members of society through the discipline of baseball. Not really Morgan's thing, but still. It was definitely dorky anime stuff. Only now did Morgan remember that when she'd first started school, she'd seen Tressa doodling an anime character in the margin of her notebook.

She gave Tressa a pained smile. "Oops. My bad."

"And like I said," continued Tressa, "if you say Joel is cool, then he's cool." She gave Hannah a hard look. "Isn't that right?"

Hannah rolled her eyes. "I guess I'll give him another chance."

"He's not going to be mean to me?" asked Piper worriedly.

"He was mean to you?" Morgan asked, surprised.

"When they were like *five*," said Tressa.

"I think he's way nicer than Jake and them," Morgan assured her.

That seemed to set her at ease. At least, as much as Piper was ever at ease.

"So what did you need to talk to Joel about on Saturday in such a hurry?" asked Hannah.

Morgan looked at them all. Should she continue this honesty streak? What was that old saying her dad liked? In for a penny, in for a pound.

"You know how you guys all thought my house was haunted when you were growing up?"

"Uh, yeah?" asked Tressa.

"That's because it is."

"Come again?" asked Hannah.

"I'm serious. That boy I asked your great-grandpa about? The reason I started researching him in the first place was because there was spooky stuff happening at my house, like, *all the time*. That boy drowned in the harbor after escaping the Nazi summer camp, and Joel thinks his ghost is still trying to get home."

They were all silent for a moment.

"You're being for real . . ." said Tressa, her expression awed.

"Yup."

Another stretch of silence.

"What kind of spooky stuff?" asked Piper.

"It started off small," said Morgan. "Just a dripping sound outside my window. Then this weird crying. And there were sandy footprints on the balcony that time—"

"Are you sure it wasn't just *Joel* messing with you?" demanded Hannah.

Morgan glared at her. "Not unless he's figured out a way to pump seawater into my plumbing."

"What's *that* mean?" asked Tressa.

"Seawater and seaweed have been coming out of every faucet. It got so bad, my dad had to shut all the water off in the house last night."

"So your parents know about this ghost?" asked Hannah.

"They don't believe me. My dad was calling plumbers this morning trying to get someone to come fix it. Like that would—"

TAP

Morgan froze.

TAP

She slowly turned toward the sound.

TAP

Water dripped from the ceiling to land with a splat on the floor directly behind her.

"Ugh, this school," said Hannah. "That roof leaks every time it rains. You'd think someone would fix it, but—"

"It's not raining," Morgan said.

"Huh?" asked Hannah.

Morgan pointed out the nearest window. The sky was overcast, but there was no rain.

TAP

All four of them stared at the small rippling puddle on the floor.

"You don't think . . ." began Tressa.

TAP

"It's probably just a leaky pipe," said Hannah.

"Yeah," said Morgan. "Probably."

She really wanted to believe that. The ghost had never bothered her during the day. Well, except when it had perched on the balcony that one afternoon. Either way, it had never haunted her anywhere except around her house.

But things were different now, so maybe nowhere was safe.

Later, Morgan stopped at the drinking fountain between classes. Without thinking, she leaned in and pressed the button.

A splash of cold, gritty seawater hit her open mouth. She coughed and spat it out, getting an unpleasant flashback from the previous night. She watched with sick horror as the cloudy water swirled down the drain.

The spout spurted, making her flinch. Then a thin strand of seaweed spilled out.

"Morgan . . ."

Piper had been waiting for the drinking fountain behind her, but now her eyes were wide as she stared at the slimy green tendril that dangled there.

Morgan spat into the drain again, still tasting the salty grit. Then she looked grimly at Piper.

"I think it's following me."

"I hope you didn't swallow, like, a ghost bug or something," said Piper.

Morgan stared at her. "*Excuse* me?"

"Oh, uh . . ." Piper's pale cheeks flushed. "I think I saw it in *Poltergeist II*? The dad is drinking a bottle of some alcohol and accidentally swallows this little ghost worm and then gets possessed by it. Eventually he throws up the worm, except it's grown much larger, and when it crawls out of his mouth—"

"I don't need to hear any more," Morgan said quickly. "Piper, I gotta say, I didn't picture you as a horror movie fan."

"I don't think they're all that scary, actually," said Piper. "Not like real-life stuff."

"Yeah, well, turns out, some of it *is* real-life stuff," said Morgan.

"I suppose that's true," admitted Piper. "Oh, sorry, I guess I made you feel even worse."

Morgan considered a moment. "Actually it's strangely comforting to know that you of all people have a macabre streak."

Piper smiled shyly. "I guess that kind of makes me a creepy weirdo too, huh?"

Morgan returned her smile. "Welcome to the party."

Piper suddenly gave her the widest grin Morgan had ever seen from her friend.

"The *ghost* party."

Morgan laughed.

Why was she laughing? There was a real ghost haunting her. She was terrified out of her mind! And here she was giggling with a friend over a joke that wasn't even very funny. Maybe because despite everything that was going on, she no longer felt alone.

CHAPTER

THIRTY

Contrary to what many anime and manga stories claimed, the power of friendship could not actually conquer all. That became painfully clear when Morgan went to the bathroom before her last class of the day.

Once she was finished, she nervously approached the line of three sinks to wash her hands. It wasn't like she could skip that part. Yuck. So she gathered her courage, then stepped resolutely toward the middle sink.

Gingerly, as though afraid of startling it, she turned the knob.

Clean water.

She breathed a quick sigh of relief, then briskly washed her hands and shut off the faucet. Feeling a little better, she walked over to the hand dryer. Then, behind her, she heard:

TAP

Morgan spun back around. The middle sink dripped in a steady rhythm.

TAP

She was certain she'd turned it all the way off. But the taps gradually became faster.

TAP-TAP-TAP-TAP-TAP

Then the water just started gushing out of the spigot. A moment later, the other two sinks started doing the same. Soon all three were spouting cold, grimy seawater.

She ran over and jiggled the knobs, but that didn't stop them. And the basins didn't seem to be draining either. In a few moments, they began overflowing, spilling out across the bathroom floor. Then there was an ominous rumble, and seawater started pouring from the toilet stalls as well. The dark, turgid water spread rapidly across the tiles until it joined with the water from the sinks. The entire floor was covered.

"Morgan, you about done?" she heard Tressa call.

The door opened and Tressa walked into the bathroom, looking mildly annoyed.

"Class is starting in—"

Then she slipped.

It was like slow motion as Morgan watched her friend's eyes stretch wide in panic while her feet skidded out from under her. Tressa fell backward, arms windmilling, her skull about to slam into the hard, wet linoleum. Morgan's thoughts flooded with Joel's warnings about all the accidents the ghost had caused . . .

Then Morgan watched in amazement as her own hand shot out and grabbed Tressa's arm, catching her before she hit the ground.

They looked at each other for a moment, their gasps nearly drowned out by the sound of gushing water.

"Thank you," whispered Tressa as Morgan helped her back to her feet.

Morgan nodded, not trusting herself to speak yet. She glanced down at the dark, ankle-deep water beneath them. She could see her own reflection, face pale and drawn, looking as frightened as she felt.

Next to her reflection was the ghost—with his rotting, bloated skin and empty eyes.

Joseph's mouth stretched wide in a silent scream. All around them, the stalls, sinks, hand dryers, and mirrors began to vibrate.

Morgan and Tressa stared at each other with terrified eyes.

The mirrors cracked, showing long, spidery lines.

Tressa let out a yelp, her face now ashen, her hands shaking.

Morgan looked back down at the water, but the ghost was gone.

"It's getting worse," she said grimly. "Come on, let's get out of here."

As she led the stunned Tressa out of the bathroom, her friend was practically babbling, her usual cool completely gone. "I-It's not that I didn't believe you, exactly. But this . . . this is . . ." Words seemed to fail her.

"Yeah," Morgan said.

After school, she headed straight for the Goddess by the Sea. Her friends volunteered to go with her, and she was grateful. Even Hannah joined them.

"I can't let these two think they're braver than me," she declared.

The skies were even darker now as Morgan and her friends hurried through downtown Port Jefferson. A chill wind had picked up, pulling at their hair and clothes.

Piper pointed to a nearby tree. The branches were twisting and bobbing up and down.

"My dad says if you can see the bottom of the leaves like that, you're in for a bad storm."

Just how bad, Morgan wasn't sure. Maybe the kind of storm that had killed Joseph Klaus.

Finally they reached the little shop with the crystals and tie-dyed clothing hanging in the window.

"This looks like some kind of hippie place," said Hannah.

"I'm pretty sure it is," said Morgan. "But the lady seemed to know what she was talking about last time, so hopefully she'll know what to do."

They entered the dimly lit store. There was still that odd sweet-spicy smell to the air, but instead of gentle harp music this time, it sounded like . . . whale song, maybe?

"Welcome, ladies," the older woman behind the counter said calmly, as though she'd been expecting them.

"The ghost came back," said Morgan.

The woman gazed at her with sharp gray eyes. "I see."

"I did the smudging, just like you said. And it seemed to work. There was nothing for, like, *weeks*. And then last night it was back, and it was *angry*."

"I'm not surprised," said the woman. "Smudging isn't a permanent solution. Pushing it away from where it wants to go probably just made its desire to get there even stronger."

"Well, what *is* a permanent solution?" demanded Morgan.

The woman's expression hardened. "Young lady, is that any way to ask for something?"

Morgan wanted to climb over the counter and shake this woman. *Didn't she realize how serious this was?* But of course, the shopkeeper probably knew better than anyone how serious it was. So Morgan forced herself to take a deep breath.

"Sorry. I'm just . . ."

She glanced back at her friends. It was embarrassing to say out loud, but there was no point trying to act cool now.

"I'm just really scared," she admitted.

The woman sighed. "Of course you are, dear. I'd be worried if you weren't. Now, why don't you tell me more about your unwelcome guest? We'll see what we can come up with."

So Morgan told her everything. From the beginning, and in more detail than she had with anyone else. The woman listened patiently without comment until Morgan was finished.

"I think I understand," she finally said. "First, do you still have the boy's uniform? The Nazi one?"

"I think so? My mom said she was going to see about donating it to a museum. But she's been really busy with work, so I don't think she'd gotten around to it yet."

"The uniform isn't necessary, but it will speed things

up," said the shopkeeper. "Go home, get the uniform, and place it in an open area in your house. Everyone who's there should gather around it. Then light the sage and keep the smoke over the uniform while you *all* chant a specific mantra."

"What mantra?" asked Morgan.

"Welcome home."

Morgan stared at her. "You're joking."

"I'm not," said the woman.

"But . . . won't that bring the ghost to me?"

The shopkeeper nodded. "It will."

"So *then* what do I do?" asked Morgan.

The woman gazed at her with those penetrating gray eyes for a moment, then suddenly smiled. "I'm sure you'll know what to do when the time comes. Just remember, there's no such thing as evil spirits."

CHAPTER

THIRTY-ONE

"*Are we really going to* do this?" Tressa asked uneasily as the four girls once again hurried through the streets.

The sky overhead had grown almost as dark as night by then, and spatters of rain were beginning to fall, hitting the back of Morgan's neck with a chilling splat.

"I guess we are," she said.

"What if that old lady doesn't know what she's talking about?" asked Hannah.

"You got a better idea?" demanded Morgan.

Hannah shrugged. "I'm just saying, maybe we

shouldn't completely trust her. Sounds like her suggestion will only make things worse."

"Yeah . . ." Morgan couldn't argue there. Welcoming the ghost seemed like the opposite of what she wanted to do.

She felt some relief when they finally got to her house. After all, the one place the ghost hadn't gone was *inside*. And Morgan's parents were home. Having them there would make the whole thing feel a little less scary.

But her relief evaporated once she stepped inside and saw her parents standing in the foyer all dressed up.

"*There* you are," her mother said. "Did you forget what day it is?"

Morgan stared at her. "Day?"

"Your mother is hosting one of her client socials at the firm tonight," said her father. "And of course she needs *me* there to charm everyone into a swoon."

"Oh . . . Right . . ."

Morgan's mom held a party for her clients every few months. In the past, it hadn't been a huge deal because the offices were in Brooklyn, just down the street from their old apartment. But now it was an hour and a half train ride away. They probably needed to leave now to get there on time, and wouldn't be back until late.

Her mother's eyes narrowed. "You're the one who said you didn't need a babysitter anymore. Are you going to be okay?"

"It's just . . ." She glanced out the door to where her friends were waiting on the porch. Usually kids weren't allowed over when there were no adults present.

"I see," said her mother.

"Oh, it'll be fine," said her father. "Weren't we just talking about how nice it was that we can count on Morgan so much?"

"True . . ." her mother admitted.

He leaned out the door to look at Morgan's friends.

"Which of you is the responsible one?"

They looked at one another in confusion, not accustomed to Morgan's dad's casual weirdness.

Finally Tressa said, "I have to wrangle my twin little brothers all the time, so I guess it's me."

"Excellent qualifications!" he declared, then looked at Morgan's mother. "Well, *I'm* convinced. How about you?"

She eyed him for a moment, then turned to Morgan. "This is a big opportunity to show us how much we can trust you, Morgan. Don't blow it."

Morgan didn't exactly want her parents gone, but she couldn't stop that from happening. And if her parents weren't going to be there, she definitely wanted her friends around.

"You've got nothing to worry about, Mom," she assured her, and really hoped that was true.

As soon as her parents were gone, Morgan hurried to their room, with the others trailing behind.

"I don't normally go through my parents' stuff," she said as she looked through their closet.

"Really?" asked Hannah. "I do it all the time."

Just as Morgan thought, her mother had jammed the uniform on a shelf in the back, which was where she always seemed to put things she didn't want to deal with. The uniform was folded in such a way that the swastika armband wasn't visible, which had probably been on purpose.

"That's it?" Tressa asked, eyeing the folded brown clothes.

Morgan wordlessly unfolded the uniform to reveal the swastika.

"Ugh!" Tressa wrinkled her nose, like it smelled.

The four of them stared at the child-sized Nazi uniform in Morgan's arms.

"That's definitely the real thing . . ." Hannah looked deeply unnerved. "And my great-grandpa wore one just like it."

Then the doorbell rang.

"That must be Joel," said Morgan as she hurried down to let him in.

"You invited a *boy* over while your parents are out?" Hannah asked, smirking.

Morgan felt herself blush. "It's not like that! But he's been with me since the beginning, so I wanted him here at the end." Her eyes narrowed. "And I expect all three of you to be nice."

"Except Hannah's never nice," pointed out Tressa.

Hannah looked genuinely offended by that. "That's not fair! I'm nice to Piper all the time, even when she's being an annoying wimp!"

"It's true," said Piper earnestly.

"Well, pretend Joel is the boy version of Piper," suggested Morgan. It wasn't actually a bad comparison. Joel was easily the most sensitive boy she'd ever met. And despite that sensitivity, Joel and Piper were both apparently drawn to dark, gory stuff like *Poltergeist* and *Carrion Flowers.*

Hannah frowned thoughtfully. "You know, treating Joel like another Piper might actually work."

"Great," said Morgan.

They hurried downstairs and Morgan pulled open the front door. Joel stood outside looking very anxious. She'd texted him that it was time to deal with the ghost once and for all—and she'd also warned him that the other girls would be there. She wondered which he found more nerve-racking.

"It's going to be fine," she told him as she pulled him into the house. Once again, she could only hope that was true.

"Yeah, don't worry, Joel," Hannah said, giving him a hearty clap on the back. "If anything happens, I'll look out for you."

He stared at her like he had no idea what was going on.

"Thanks . . . ?" he ventured.

"Joel." Morgan held out the uniform for him to see.

He turned toward her, still looking utterly baffled by the lack of hostility from the girls. But then his eyes fixed on the swastika, and everything else seemed to fall away.

"There it is," he said quietly, then shivered.

"Again, we're really going to do this?" asked Tressa. "Purposefully summon the ghost to us?"

"I don't know how reliable any of it is," said Joel. "But pretty much all the occult stuff I read online says you have to call forth the ghost before you can banish it."

"That's how it is in most movies," agreed Piper.

"Uh-huh," said Tressa, not looking any more at ease. "And just how do we *banish* it?"

They all looked at Morgan. She forced a smile.

"The shopkeeper said I'll know what to do when the time comes."

"Oh, this is going to go great," said Hannah.

CHAPTER

THIRTY-TWO

Was it merely coincidence that the storm began in earnest just as they gathered around the uniform? Morgan wanted to think so, but couldn't quite convince herself. The sky outside was now completely black, so they had to turn on the lights just to see. Rain fell against the windows in a steady hiss, and thunder rumbled in the distance.

They laid out the uniform and sat around it in a circle—Morgan, then Joel, Hannah, Tressa, and Piper. Morgan took out the smudge stick she'd used before, which still had plenty left. Joel struck a match and lit it for her. Then she held it over the uniform.

She watched the thick, curling tongue of smoke drift up for a moment.

"All together," she said. "Ready?"

They nodded.

"Welcome home."

Even with all their voices in unison, they sounded shaky. Unsure.

"We have to keep doing it," said Joel.

"Welcome home."

Why this phrase? Morgan wondered. It all went back to what Joel had said at the very beginning. That for over eighty years, this ghost has been trying to get home.

"Welcome home."

Not just *any* home, but a place he felt safe. He'd been stuck at that Nazi summer camp, forced to work, told he had to hate people, and trained to overthrow the American government. That was already bad enough.

"Welcome home."

In addition to all that, the other kids had bullied him because he couldn't pretend to be awful like them. He'd probably even *tried* to be like them, or at least not draw attention to himself, and failed. Which had made it worse. So they'd made fun of him and beat him.

"Welcome home."

And then that girl, Tillie Koch, had stood up to them all and died because of it. Did he know her? Even if he hadn't, it must have been terrifying. He must have felt so alone and frightened.

"Welcome home."

It had been a long drive from Yaphank to Port Jefferson. How had he escaped? How had he gotten all this way? Had the Nazis chased him? Even if they hadn't, he must have been so tired, hungry, and miserable. Morgan couldn't imagine having the courage to do what he did, all alone.

"Welcome home."

Worst of all, he'd come all this way only to perish. Maybe his home had even been in sight when the storm had pulled him down into that cold, dark water. To have traveled so far, suffered so much, and then to die so horribly . . .

"Welcome home."

A streak of lightning snaked across the sky, followed immediately by the crack of thunder. The storm was right on top of them now. Rain hammered the windows so hard it rattled the panes. But it wasn't merely rain any longer—chunks of ice the size of marbles pounded the glass.

"Welcome home."

Through the curtain of hail, Morgan saw the wind bend trees nearly sideways. A boat had been torn from its mooring and careened wildly through the harbor until it smashed into the dock. Morgan had never seen a storm like this. Had she and her friends caused this? No, it couldn't be . . .

"Welcome home."

TAP

Despite the roar of the storm, she heard it.

TAP

Morgan turned toward a nearby window. Water dripped from the sill onto the floor.

TAP

"Welcome home."

Joel touched Morgan's shoulder, then pointed.

A pool of water was spreading out from underneath the front door.

"Welcome home."

She heard a sputter from the kitchen. Seawater began spurting out of the sink, even though the faucet was shut off. She heard similar sounds from upstairs, probably every faucet in the house going all at once.

"Should we stop?" shouted Hannah over the noise.

"No! Keep going!" Morgan didn't know why, but she felt there was something more they needed to do.

"Welcome home."

There was another flash of lightning and boom of thunder overhead, but this time it was accompanied by an explosive pop, like a firework. Then the lights flickered out. They were left in the dark, their faces lit only by the smoldering red of the smudge stick in Morgan's hand. The wind blew so hard that the old house shuddered and groaned, as if it might be torn from its foundation any minute.

"Welcome home."

A chunk of hail struck the window with such force it cracked the glass.

"Welcome home."

The front door shook, as though someone were rattling the handle from the outside.

"Welcome home."

Then the screaming began. Not soft and despairing, or even ragged and desperate any longer. These were shrieks of pure rage—the fury of a hurricane given voice.

"It's him . . ." Joel's voice was barely audible beneath the storm and shrieks.

"We have to stop!" shouted Tressa.

"This ghost is homicidal!" agreed Hannah.

But Morgan knew the ghost wasn't homicidal. It was just frantic to feel safe. To feel comforted. To be let in from the endless cold.

She handed the sage to Joel. "Keep going."

He bit his lip, nodded, then said loudly, "Welcome home!"

Morgan stood up in the darkness, then turned to the shuddering front door.

"Welcome home!" This time Piper joined Joel.

Morgan walked slowly over to the door and placed her hand on it. She could feel it vibrating with pressure, like it might blow off its hinges at any moment.

"What are you *doing*?" screamed Hannah. "Don't open that door! It's going to *kill* us!"

But Morgan understood now. Like the woman at the shop said, there was no such thing as evil spirits. This was just a boy named Joseph Klaus who had been sad and lonely, and who wanted more than anything to go home. There was only one thing Morgan could do.

She gripped the handle.

"Morgan! No!" shouted Tressa.

"Don't do it!" yelled Hannah.

But Morgan threw open the door and thrust out her arms. The wind, rain, and hail buffeted her so hard that she had to close her eyes. But she held firm, hands outstretched.

"Welcome home, Joseph," she whispered. "You can finally rest."

And then it stopped.

The shrieks, the wind, the rain, everything.

Morgan opened her eyes. The black storm clouds slowly parted, showing a sliver of blue sky beyond. The sun shone through the gap, and all the threatening rain and hail now glittered on leaves and grass like crystals. The turbulent harbor across the street sparkled like a bed of jewels.

It was possibly the most beautiful thing she had ever seen.

When she turned back to her friends, she was grinning from ear to ear.

"Is . . . it over?" asked Joel.

She shrugged. "I don't know if he's gone, but at least he's not unhappy anymore."

CHAPTER

THIRTY-THREE

At the end of the final volume of *My Secret Dream of a Boring Life*, Zophia Zye, the Night Queen, brought peace between her kingdom and the Undead Kingdom of Nezhit. She didn't even need to destroy King Srogi to do it. After all, the gift that the mysterious wandering god had given her wasn't incredible magic power—it was the ability to read and comprehend anything. Not strength, but *understanding*. That was how, time and again, the loneliest person in the kingdom was able to bring people together, humans and oni, elves and dwarves, even the living and the dead.

Morgan knew what she had done wasn't nearly as cool. But when she sat in the ice-cream shop with Joel, Hannah, Tressa, and Piper, everyone talking and laughing, it felt close enough.

Her parents hadn't been mad about the flooding or the cracked windowpane. In fact, they'd been impressed with how well she'd handled herself during the record-breaking storm that had struck Port Jefferson. The worst storm on record since 1937, the news said.

Professor Johnson had been appreciative to accept Joseph's old uniform for the Port Jefferson Historical Society, noting that even the shameful parts of history should be documented and preserved. Especially the shameful parts. He even spoke of working with a similar group in Yaphank to organize some sort of exhibit. That really made Morgan happy, because more than anything, she wanted people to know that Nazis weren't just some faraway problem. They were something that happened right there in America.

And then there was the ghost, Joseph Klaus. Morgan never again heard the crying or dripping. There were no more problems with the plumbing. Once, Joel had asked her if she thought that meant Joseph was gone for good. She wasn't so sure. Maybe he'd become like Zsa Zsa, who had once been an angry spirit, but thanks to Zophia Zye had become a heroic frost spirit who was always happy to help her out. Maybe Joseph would be a happy ghost now, watching out for her. Or maybe he went to be with his family, wherever they were.

Either way, Morgan didn't feel out of place on Long Island anymore. When the first episode of the *My Secret Dream of a Boring Life* anime came out, she decided to throw a party to watch it. She even invited Madison. She honestly hadn't really expected a response at all. Or at best, that maybe Madison would watch online along with them. So she was surprised when her mom actually brought her all the way out to Port Jefferson for it.

Morgan's dad made four different flavors of popcorn: butter, cheese, caramel, and chili lime, all with natural ingredients and no microwave. He might be a terrible cook in general, but he was a popcorn genius. Then the adults disappeared to leave Morgan, Madison, Joel, Tressa, Piper, and even Hannah to cluster around the couch and watch the first episode of the Night Queen anime.

Morgan's eyes sparkled while she watched Zophia Zye in her human form, eyes blazing as she glared at the well-meaning but clueless Kosuke.

*"We shall see how well this human under-
stands the circumstances once I turn this entire
meadow to ash!"*

Hannah let out a bark of laughter. "I like this girl already!"

It became a weekly thing for the Long Islanders, and even though Madison couldn't come every weekend, she watched online with them for the entire season. Morgan knew that she and Madison would never have the friendship they once did, but that was okay. People grew and changed, and that was okay too.

In fact, when summer came around the following year, Morgan actually got pretty good at wakeboarding.

AUTHOR'S NOTE

· · · · · · · · · · · · · · · · ·

Most of the characters in this book are fictional, including Joseph Klaus. Tragically, however, Tillie Koch was real, and really died because the youth director at Camp Siegfried, Theodore Dinkelacker, refused to allow a doctor to treat her.

Tillie's friend, Helen Vooros, was also real. She survived both Camp Siegfried and Camp Nordland, and was then sent to Germany to train with the Hitler Youth. She made it through all of that, and when she was finally able to return to America and escape the German American Bund, she gave testimony before the Special Committee on Un-American Activities in Congress that helped bring the leaders of the organization to justice. In fact, a lot of the research about Camp Siegfried that was included in this novel came directly from the transcripts of her testimony. So thank you, Helen, for your courage and honesty.

I should also thank the Port Jefferson Visitors Center

and the real Port Jefferson Historical Society, both of which were friendly and helpful during my research trip. Also, my apologies for taking so many liberties with your fair city in the service of narrative.

While I relied mostly on primary sources like Helen's testimony before Congress, I also found *Hitler's American Friends* by Bradley W. Hart and *Swastika Nation* by Arnie Bernstein helpful for context. The New York City Department of Records and Information Services was also very helpful in providing some truly chilling images of American Nazis on Long Island.

Thanks also to the Long Island contingent of my family: Laura Kelley, Peter Dodge, Alexander Berger, Tia Henry, Elizabeth Berger, Danny Stern, and of course my favorite cousin and fellow writer, Maya Edwards.

Lastly thanks to my editor, Zachary Clark; my agent, Jill Grinberg; the whole team at JGLM; and my sons, Logan and Zane, for their continued and unrelenting support.

Chapter 4

INTO THE WILD

O nce Zsa Zsa and I teleported to the human forest, I knew I'd made the right choice. We walked beneath the trees with pleasantly warm sunlight filtering through the branches and a bed of pine needles underfoot. A gentle breeze caressed my soft human cheeks, bringing with it the scent of flowers and lush greenery that lifted my spirits even further.

This was the counterbalance to having such a delicate body, I supposed. Its sensual delights were far more pronounced.

I walked lightly amongst the trees, excitement reverberating through my chest. It felt as though all my cares and worries had been left behind at the palace. And in a way, they had. My generals could surely handle things for a few weeks. I might have grown so accustomed to the burden of leadership that I had forgotten its weight. But by the goddess was it nice to have that load lifted for a little while. The feeling was almost intoxicating.

Zsa Zsa was curled up on my shoulder in his new kitten shape, making an odd little rumbling sound. He looked rather like a ball of fluff. When I reached my fleshy human hand up to touch him, I found him quite pleasant to stroke.

"Do we have any idea where we're going, my queen?" he asked sleepily.

"I doubt it matters," I said. "Humans are so plentiful, we're certain to come across one of their settlements eventually."

"And then what will you do?"

"I'm not quite sure," I admitted. "Insert ourselves into their community somehow so we can learn more about my new subjects. It can't be that complicated. They are just humans, after all."

We continued through the forest until we reached a large, flowery meadow. The cacophony of scents was quite wonderful.

"Why don't we have flowers at the palace, Zsa Zsa?"

"I believe they require sunlight, oh Queen of Night."

"Hm, I suppose that's true. Surely we could enchant some room or other to have sunlight."

"I have no doubt you could, though it may be more complicated to explain to your generals why you would."

"I don't need to explain *anything* to my generals, Zsa Zsa."

"Of course not, my queen."

Then I heard a low growl nearby, followed by another, and then another. Soon the sound was all around us. A pack of wolflings rose from their hiding places behind trees and out of the tall grassy meadow. Wolflings looked like werewolves, but had the size and brains of regular wolves. They generally ran in packs of ten to twenty, and through sheer numbers could overwhelm prey much larger than themselves.

I watched with bemusement as they began to slowly encircle us.

"What on earth are they doing?" I asked.

"I believe they intend to attack you, my queen."

"Really?"

"It appears that way."

"I suppose that means my disguise is effective."

"Indisputably."

I watched their gleaming eyes and slavering jaws with amusement. "Still, I think even their tiny little teeth would harm this delicate form."

"I suspect they would, Your Majesty."

"I can't very well have it mangled before I've even met any humans."

"It would not be an ideal introduction," he agreed.

"So I suppose I'll need to do something about these impertinent pups."

"Please do, Your Majesty. They offend my delicate kitten nose."

"This new form of yours is growing on me," I admitted. "In fact, that nose is rather precious."

He squinted at me with pleasure. "Isn't it, though?"

I sighed and squared my shoulders. "Very well, let's handle these poor little brutes."

While I didn't expect it would take much to drive them off, I was feeling so cheerful and energetic that I decided to cast the Malevolent Fury of Night's Visage on them. It was overkill, but surely I deserved to have a little fun.

Then, just as I was about to begin the short incantation that would shred the scruffy wretches to strips of fur, an arrow flew past me and embedded in the eye of one of the wolflings.

I turned in the direction the arrow had come from and saw a small group of humans sprinting across the meadow toward us.

"Don't worry, miss!" a burly brown-haired male called to me. "We'll save you!"

I gaped at them.

"Did they just . . . ?"

"I believe they did, my queen."

I watched the humans draw closer. Two males, one female, and one that seemed perhaps both. Or neither. I didn't really know how many genders humans had. The burly male who had spoken so presumptuously was wielding a large war hammer. Well, large for a human, I supposed. The female, who had curly red hair, held the bow that had so rudely interrupted my incantation. The other-gendered one had black hair slicked back, and they wielded a pair of curved daggers that I thought looked quite nice, but of little combat value.

The last member of the party, male, veered over to me while the others headed straight for the wolflings. He was slim, with shaggy black hair, refined features, and an earnest expression.

"Hey, miss! Can you use a sword?" he called.

I wasn't sure what he was getting at. "Yes, I have had some instruction in swordsmanship . . ."

"Great! Feel free to help out!"

Then he tossed a small sword at my feet.

I looked down at the blade. It was easily the most pathetic weapon I'd ever seen. The craftsmanship was subpar, and it had not been well maintained. The binding was frayed, and the flimsy steel was edged with rust.

Then I looked back at the human, who was smiling innocently at me.

"He's serious," I muttered to Zsa Zsa. "He actually thinks he's helping me."

"So it would seem, my queen."

"And now he's waiting for . . . *gratitude?*"

"That would be traditional under the circumstances as he understands them, Your Majesty."

"We shall see how well he understands the *circumstances* once I turn this entire meadow to ash!"

I decided I would show this foolish human just how much of an insult his pathetic sword was. I began to cast the tenth-tier spell Incandescent Blaze of Lava's Birth. My hands rose to form the intricate movements, and my mouth opened to speak the prayer to Kagutsuchi the fire god.

"I hate to interrupt when you're in such a beautifully righteous rage, my queen," Zsa Zsa said mildly. "But I suspect that once you cast a spell in the lost language of the gods, this human and his companions will no longer believe you to be one of them, and everything we have done to get to this point will have been for naught."

"But I can't just let him think he's *saving* me," I protested. "As though I'm some helpless *child*."

"In that case," said Zsa Zsa, "perhaps you should use the sword he has provided after all."

I looked down at the sad little blade again and sighed. "I suppose I will."

When I picked it up, I could immediately feel its meager and unbalanced heft. Then I glanced over at the human.

He nodded enthusiastically. "That's the spirit!"

He drew his own sword and hurried to join his companions.

I watched the humans battle the wolflings for a moment. They were reasonably skilled and worked well as a team. They called to one another, cheering their comrades on and protecting their blind spots. Their diverse specializations complemented one another's weaknesses. It was clear that there was a strong companionship amongst them. It was the sort of bond I'd always found appealing but had never been able to achieve, not even with my generals.

"It does look fun," I admitted.

Zsa Zsa hopped off my shoulder and bowed his fluffy little head. "You never know until you try, Your Majesty."

"Indeed."

I looked down at my sword speculatively and pursed my lips. "Surely a *small* enchantment wouldn't give us away."

"I think it unlikely, my queen."

I pressed two fingers to the hilt. As I slid my fingers up the flat side of the dull, nicked blade, I whispered in the lost language of the gods, "Mother Night, I beg you, imbue this humble steel with your cutting darkness."

For a moment the blade flickered with a dark purple glow. After that, it was all but impossible to discern such a minor enchantment.

"That's a bit better." I hefted the sword. "Let's see what I remember from Abyssal Academy."

"I look forward to it, Your Majesty."

By then the humans seemed to be having some trouble with the wolflings. There were quite a lot of the little brutes, and even weaklings could overwhelm if their numbers were great enough. The burly brown-haired male human had received a substantial bite wound on his shoulder, impairing the force of his war hammer. The redheaded female had been forced into close-quarters combat with a small pack of them, putting her archery at a disadvantage. The other-gendered one darted amongst them, easily avoiding injury. But their daggers, though attractive, did little more than slow the enemy down. The male with the sword was fighting with astonishing recklessness. He appeared to be trying to carve his way over to the wounded brown-haired male, who was now beset by a large number of wolflings.

"Hang on, Riku! I'm coming!" he shouted.

It was clear he would not reach the burly male named Riku in time.

While this Riku had insulted me, it had clearly been unintentional, so I reluctantly decided to forgive him. I suspected I would have to do a lot of that in the days to come.

"Riku!" I shouted. "To your left!"

He barely managed to fend off the wolfling who lunged at his flank, but it allowed me enough time to reach him before he received further injury. My human feet were pleasantly nimble as they raced through the tall grass, and though my legs were not strong, my frame was exceptionally light, so I could easily leap over the cluster of wolflings that separated me from Riku.

He gave me a surprised look as I landed beside him. But there was little time for discussion—the wolflings closed in. Instead we stood back-to-back and fended off the onslaught. My light blade flickered through the air, severing the head of one wolfling, then piercing the brain of another.

"Miss!"

Riku slammed his hammer into the chest of one, sending it hurling toward me, dazed and helpless. I smoothly sliced it in half, its innards spraying into the air in a most satisfying way. He continued to serve them up to me like that. It almost became a game between us.

"Ha! This is teamwork!" I shouted.

Even through his evident pain and exhaustion, Riku seemed amused by my enthusiasm. "It is indeed, miss."

By that time, the other male had made his way over to us. He gazed wonderingly at me.

"I didn't know that old blade had it in her."

"Use your eyes, Kosuke!" said Riku. "It's not the sword, but the swordswoman! I've heard a true master can turn a blade of grass into a weapon that can cut steel! After seeing her in action, I think she needed little help from us in dealing with these curs."

With that statement, Riku entirely exonerated himself in my eyes.

I turned back to our prey with renewed excitement. Swordswoman? Me? Well, why not? I'd always thought there was a certain gallantry to the vocation. If a minor enchantment and my meager training at the academy qualified me for such a title amongst humans, it would be fun to pretend for a little while.

With Riku and Kosuke fighting at my side, we easily fended off the bulk of the wolfling pack while the other two humans harried their flanks, forcing them toward us and picking off those who attempted to flee. In short order, we had dispatched the lot of them.

"What a lovely diversion!" I exclaimed, enjoying the thrum of my pulse and the quickness of my breath.

Riku chuckled as he mopped the wolfling blood from his face. "What's your name, miss?"

I froze. I needed a human name. What did human names sound like? Quickly! I needed to come up with something, because obviously I shouldn't need to pause and think about my own name.

"It's Gwendolyn."

Riku's thick eyebrows rose. "An unusual name, Gwendolyn."

Drat. The only human to be named in the old texts of the gods was Gwendolyn, so it was the first one that came to mind. But of course, humans probably didn't even *know* those texts.

"It sounds western," said the female. "You do look like a westerner with that yellow hair."

"Oh yes," I said quickly. "We hail from the west."

"We?" asked the one with slicked black hair.

I pointed to Zsa Zsa, who sat demurely nearby in the grass.

The female gave an odd squeak and ran over to him with outstretched arms. Zsa Zsa watched her rapid approach with growing alarm, but thankfully did not tear her face off when she scooped him up and began to nuzzle him in an astonishingly familiar way.

"This is your kitty?" she cooed. "He's *adorable*! What's his name?"

"Oh . . ."

Dear goddess, I really hadn't thought this whole human identity plan through, had I? I had no idea what sort of name suited a kitten. Frankly I still wasn't certain what function kittens even served in human society other than as something pleasant to touch.

"He looks quite young," said Kosuke. "Have you not named him yet?"

"Er, right, not yet," I admitted. "I was thinking . . . perhaps Zsa Zsa?"

"I love it!" the red-haired female declared as she rejoined the group, poor Zsa Zsa still squashed in her embrace. She rested her chin on top of Zsa Zsa's head and grinned at me. "I'm Akari, by the way. And it looks like you've already met Riku and Kosuke. The aloof and stylish one over there is Ren."

Akari indicated the one with slicked black hair.

"Hey." Ren nodded in a rather disinterested way as they sharpened one of their daggers.

"Don't worry, they're like that with everyone at first,"

Akari interjected. "But they warm up after a while. Don't you, Ren?"

Ren shrugged, still working on the dagger. "If you say so."

"So, um, Gwendolyn . . ." Kosuke's gaze was unrelentingly sincere as he looked at me. There was something about it that made me feel as though he really *cared* about me, even though he'd just met me. It was unnerving, but also oddly enjoyable. In fact, I felt my human cheeks flush with warmth as I watched him struggle to say whatever he was about to say. It seemed as though it was vital to him that he express it in the best possible way. But why? He didn't even know I was the Night Queen. Why did I matter to him?

"Yes?" I prompted him.

"I was just—I mean *we* were just . . ." He glanced around at his companions and none contradicted him. "Well, where are you headed?"

"I'm not sure," I confessed.

"Ah!" said Riku. "Is this your first time traveling to the eastern lands?"

"Yes, it is." I had been completely unaware of this

whole east-west separation amongst humans, but it was proving extremely useful.

"Well then, you probably don't know your way around at all!" said Akari, still squeezing poor, suffering Zsa Zsa.

"True," I admitted.

"Perhaps you will permit us to show you around, then?" Kosuke asked eagerly.

"I would appreciate it."

"That's great! Just great!"

They all smiled at one another. And while I was not exactly sure why, I found myself smiling as well. This whole companionship thing was really quite strange. But so far, I had to admit I rather liked it.

Then I saw the pleading look in Zsa Zsa's eyes.

"Er, Akari?"

"Hmm?" she asked, her face nuzzled into Zsa Zsa's fluffy neck.

"I'm afraid Zsa Zsa's tolerance for . . . *cuddling* is not high."

"Oh, dear. Well, that's a shame." She handed him to me. "I'll just have to take what I can get."

"Perhaps he will acclimate in time." I gave him a meaningful glance as he moved to his perch on my shoulder. Surely he understood that the more favorably these humans viewed us, the better our chances at full integration would be.

He gave me a steady look, then sighed, rested his chin on his paws, and closed his eyes. I chose to see that as an indication of weary resignation.

"Wonderful." Then I turned to my new companions. "Now, where shall we go?"

ABOUT THE AUTHOR

Kelley Skovron is the author of *Hacker's Key* and the G.I. Joe Classified series for kids, as well as books for teens and adults. They live just outside Washington, DC, with a cat, a dog, and a teenager, so there's never a dull moment. Find them online at kelleyskovron.com.